Dead End Road

"...we hate not evil except for the love we have for good..."

St. Frances de Sales

Dead End Road

by

M. J. Lunsen

Published by Oxbow

To Loren who listened

and

To Tim who told

Contents

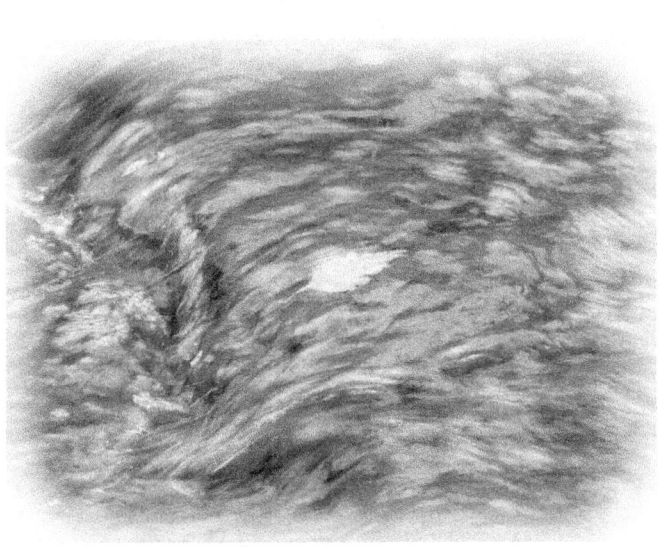

Part 1

Josie

McDonald County

MAYBE IT'S LIKE APPALACHIA, like West Virginia, or rural Kentucky or Tennessee. Or maybe like the bayous or parts of the deep south. It's possible there are places like it all over the country, places where near mansions sit side-by-side with near huts, which sit beside houses transplanted straight from suburbia; small rural areas where people who don't know where their next meal is coming from are on very amiable and neighborly terms with people who have financial advisors to manage their assets. Or maybe this mix happens only in the southern edge of the Missouri Ozarks where it meets the hills of Arkansas.

In the far southwest corner of Missouri, winding through valleys, at the feet of steep bluffs, shaded by oak and hickory and walnut trees, creeks run clear and fast. Gravel roads run dusty and slow alongside them. Farther back, narrow dirt lanes branch off the gravel roads giving access to driveways of every description, quality, and length. Often the road itself, at some imperceptible point, becomes a driveway and a dead end.

Nature's pace in these parts is fast – as in snake-strikes and tornadoes. The affairs of the folks who live here proceed at a more gradual pace – as in porch-sitting, tea-sipping, and drawls. Yet they suit one another, this little piece of the world and the folks who settled here. But there never were large numbers of such individuals. Most people looking for someplace to settle in the 1930's, chose someplace else, someplace that offered greater assurance of not starving to death, someplace where money flowed. There was no money in McDonald County then; and there's not much more now – and for exactly the same reasons. Poor access by road and non-existent access by water keeps big manufacturing out. Marginal ground, untillable and barely fertile, keeps big agriculture out. A sparse population of low education and technical skills keeps big business out. Nothing big ever touched this part of the world.

Even in the early days, from the time of the Trail of Tears, through the Oklahoma Land Rush, and the Dustbowl days – all three right next door – on through WWI, the Great Depression, and WWII, nothing big happened, no history was made in McDonald County – which is not the same as to say no lives were lived in this out of the way place. There were a handful of people still looking for a place to be after all the good land in the country had already been taken, tilled, and turned to profit. Like Josie's parents, others on their own dirt road, still a wagon trails in those days, there were folks whose needs were small, folks who could appreciate creeks and bluffs and hardwood forests, folks who had nowhere else to go. They settled and built – and they were fruitful and multiplied as the Good Book directed – and the little roads, in due time, became neighborhoods, some rightly considered Sodoms or Gomorrahs, and nearly all evolving into hillbilly versions of Babel as time went by and families grew and building styles changed until it became the unholy mess it is today.

The people who settled here were do-it-yourselfers – mostly of necessity – and like today, there were those of greater and lesser skill, those owning to higher and lower standards, those of adequate and less-than-adequate means, and those who were flamboyantly creative; the latter sometimes for the best and sometimes for the worst; and any and all combinations of these. And so it continued for many decades and still does today.

In this part of the country, the neighborhoods are not like those of small towns and big cities, where an entire area assumes a single aggregate personality, from which is given a single impression formed by the equal spacing, common age, average cost, and shared architectural aesthetics of rows upon rows of houses and yards. The visual commonalities of these urban habitats, for good or ill, rightly or wrongly, inevitably shape an outsider's perception of the inhabitants in terms of likely incomes, occupations, hobbies, and educational levels.

Rather, on these rural county dead end roads, nearest neighbors are sometimes a mile or more distant from one another; and sometimes nearest neighbors are close enough to smell each other's suppers. The houses range from the newly built to those with a century or more of history. Within each age category, there are houses worth many hundreds of thousands of dollars and houses whose value would barely justify the cost of having them bulldozed to the ground. Given these attributes, it is not surprising that there is no common architectural aesthetic, no sense of style, place, or purpose, and nothing at all in the way of consistency, correspondence, or complementarity.

There are homes with ten foot tall wrought iron gates between brick pillars, through which asphalt driveways lead to new five thousand square foot houses. Four-car garages, twenty-stall horse barns, indoor riding arenas, and the occasional tennis court are scattered about meticulously landscaped acreages. It's cheap to build here and easy to look richer than you are. The rich people are usually politicians or retirees, those who have made their money elsewhere and brought it with them, because even small piles of money are fortunes here.

There are ranch style homes, split levels, and modular homes, all of varying ages and quality. These mostly have mowed yards, and are variously equipped with swing sets and trampolines, or metal pole buildings and gas powered conveyances of every imaginable age and type, or a smattering of accessory buildings used as greenhouses, chicken coops, or housing for animals – anything from a family milk cow to emus and llamas. They are the homes of the middle class, encompassing a broad spectrum of means, interests, and inclinations toward maintenance. The folks in the middle work at low paying jobs in feed mills or grocery stores, a few driving far enough to work at a Walmart in the nearby towns large enough to support one.

There are rusted trailer houses, school buses and semi-truck trailers turned into living quarters. There are tar paper shacks, old campers, and structures whose original purpose can barely be ascertained, their identities as tiny churches, one room school houses, town halls, and gas stations obscured by decades of neglect and hidden by slowly advancing accretions of scrub forest and rusted junk. Truly, every imaginable type of enclosure big enough to shelter a stained and lumpy mattress is inhabited by someone. Many of these dwellings want for amenities such as on-site water, electricity, and like conveniences, their longtime residents lacking the means to pay for them or to make other choices with regard to living arrangements. For the most part, they live in these dilapidated and repurposed structures on ground paid for by forgotten great-grandparents; and they have neither known nor hankered for anything else. Perhaps more so than any other residents – more so than the affluent or the middle class – they are in a place they profoundly consider home. As for this majority, most are on some sort of government assistance, either lawfully or not. Many earn a little cash cutting wood for others or doing the occasional odd jobs. Some deal drugs. These last, these bottom-rungers, the poorest, are of the greatest concentration on many a dead end road in the part of the country known as McDonald County, Missouri.

In fact, every kind of person lives on these roads. There are hookers, druggies, ordinary working folks, old people, con artists, and thieves. There are residents who aren't right in the head – some crazy, some slow, some burnt up druggies. There are folks who harbor evil souls and folks who have good hearts. There are people who live in tarpaper shacks and have dozens of coffee cans stuffed with hundred dollar bills. There are people who live in beautiful homes but can't find two cents to rub together. There are a few prostitutes, some fences, maybe a couple of murderers who have done their time, and a handful of hermits, grumpy and otherwise. Still, the majority are good people, compassionate because they know trouble and heartache, willing to help out a neighbor when they can. The population is about evenly split between those who fell from someplace higher and those who have never known anything else. Everyone knows everyone else's history and no one cares much. As neighborhoods, they are no more lawless than a lot of places, the only difference being that here the names of the thieves and druggies are common knowledge. The people who are not poor fear becoming so, and the poor fear dying – if they fear anything at all. They have very little else to lose. In general, they prefer not to be hassled by the cops, but many of them have grown more or less accustomed to it.

If a resident reports something stolen, the law rounds up the usual suspects – which are those who are easiest to find and arrest, not necessarily those most likely to have stolen. Some of these suspects have developed the habit of running to the woods and hiding till things blow over. Nothing is ever recovered and no one is ever charged. Thievery is the least of the ills in these neighborhoods and few people have anything of great value to be stolen, or, alternatively they have insurance or the means to replace something.

Off the highways, away from I-44 or Highway 71, off an exit and a side road, after several miles and two or three more turns, there is a world apart from cities, suburbia, historic downtowns, and anyplace where agriculture is a profitable enterprise. This is McDonald County.

MONROE AND GOLDIE AND A LITTLE GIRL

MONROE MANSELL HAD WORKED through thirty years in Oklahoma and Texas, first as a cowhand, then as a roustabout, and saved his money, not because he was economical, but because there wasn't anything he'd been interested in spending it on. By the Depression Era standards he'd lived through, he'd done well. He ate and he slept, he worked and he wandered. And then, all of a sudden it seemed, he'd gotten tired. It was as if the fact that he'd lived nearly a half century changed his concept of his life. Monroe yearned for normal things, steady things, peaceful things. He wanted to live where it was greener, where trees grew older than people do, often passing that century mark. He wanted to build his own house and live in it. He wanted to feel settled.

When he happened across a forest cut clean through with a shaded creek – by turns rumbling over rocks or meandering along, good clear water – soft and pure in the mouth – it felt so much like the home he was meant to have that he took nearly every cent three decades of work had produced, and bought a full section of land and the length of Big Sugar Creek that ran through it. He set out to build a house upon it.

Monroe was a man only slightly over average in building skill, and perhaps slightly below average in means, having spent most of his money on the ground itself, but he rose to a higher level by sheer determination, slow, hard, steady work, and a willingness to recognize and correct a shortcoming or a failure. All of his values and measures for a job well done related to sturdiness and longevity. It wasn't that he was blind to beauty; it was that he found solid construction beautiful.

For Monroe, it was about the trees – the strength, the toughness, the power of trees. It was with an eye toward the timelessness of trees that Monroe built. For the sake of the past, he chose for harvest red oaks of ample girth and height, acknowledging both that they had lived a long, long time, and that nothing lived forever. For the sake of the future, he chose for harvest red oaks with younger trees nearby that could fill the canopy when their older brothers were laid down. For the sake of the present, he chose for harvest red oaks straight, solid and close by to the site of the home he envisioned, a home which would stand long after he was gone.

Then, with the smell of sawdust and chinking still fresh, as he used to tell it, he discovered gold, right there in the Ozarks, where no one had thought to look. He'd make a sly little smile and wink at his wife. His wife's name was Golden. She was blond, petite, alone in the world, almost as quiet natured as Monroe himself, and thirty years his junior. They never seemed to notice the age difference. They had a tad over forty years together. More than that, they had a lifetime together. And a lifetime is a lifetime. Length has nothing at all to do with it.

They so cherished one another that the birth of their only child, Ella Josephine, barely made a ripple in their lives, surprise though she was. By 1951, the year of her birth, Monroe, in his sixties, was almost an old man; and Goldie, entering her forties, was no longer a young woman. Both were old enough to be grandparents, and it was grandparent kindliness they felt for their daughter, providing her with everything their simple views deemed warranted, but allowing her little penetration into the lives they'd built as a childless couple. Josie never resented it. To her it seemed a natural thing, a thing to be desired and sought, a truth upon which the whole world turned, a world within a world where two people in love would have eyes forever focused only on one another.

History flowed around McDonald County, not through it. Even at that, major events, or so it seemed, were not occurring in the world in the fifties and sixties. The shadows of the Civil Rights Movement did not extend so far as McDonald County. The question of racism never arose because there were no people of color there. The question of why that might so be never arose either. The Vietnam War, acknowledged as such, was on the horizon, but had not yet arrived. Those eligible for the draft rarely signed up because it was an inconvenient government paperwork issue, and many of those eligible either didn't know they were, didn't know what to do about it, didn't know how to write, or sometimes all three. The Cold War, for those who were aware of it, seemed a trivial matter, given the common sense recognition that if the Soviets actually did send a bomb, it would be to do more damage than was possible in Mac County. Surely the aim would be for some big city on one of the coasts. And really, what else was happening? The world outside Mac County was hidden by a cloud of "that has nothing to do with us". The local print media concerned itself mostly with obituaries, weddings, auctions, and legal listings. The hills themselves only reluctantly admitted television and radio signal in those days; and besides, those devices, as well as telephones, were as scare as they were unaffordable in those parts.

It was not surprising then, that Josie had so little memory of her childhood. There had been no event, in the wider world or even locally, that might serve as an anchor for memory. All in all, Josie's had been a childhood of evenness, devoid of passion or strife. No demands were placed upon her and she received neither praise nor criticism. She wandered the woods alone, or with a dog, first on foot, then, when she got older, on horseback. She had neither siblings nor neighborhood playmates and didn't miss them. At school, she was unremarkable – solitary rather than shy, reasonably bright, steadfastly responsible, but certainly not a superstar. None of her classmates would remember her, nor did she remember them. Home was the house her father built. It just happened to be in Mac County. And as a child, there certainly didn't seem to be anything remarkable about either one.

Josie's childhood home was situated on one particular road, known as Rural Route 5, as addresses were styled in those days, though there was nothing especially particular about it for those parts throughout her childhood and for many long years after she left it for wider vistas. It was a dead end road, a sparsely graveled, sepia dusted road pockmarked with ruts, potholes, and protruding flint, a road that stumbled up and down hills for about five miles before it petered out to a dirt lane and a vague dead end. Those who went on horseback or motorcycles didn't acknowledge the dead end, but took the lane an additional two miles as a back door to the paved county roads just west and the two lane highway beyond. Mule drawn wagons with experienced mules and drivers could make it, too, as long as it hadn't rained recently and the wagons weren't too heavily loaded.

Over the years, Rural Route 5 grew to include fifteen or twenty mailboxes scattered at random distances from one another. There were clusters of inexpensive, but carefully lettered and maintained boxes, on a single support for a small acreage that bore the modest house of the original owners surrounded by modular homes and trailer houses of their married offspring. Groups of single boxes were separated by only dozens of yards, and some mailboxes were a mile distant from their nearest neighbor. There were elaborate constructions on brick pillars, posts set in old milk cans with flowers planted around the base, rusty boxes with rusty doors barely clinging to splintered posts no longer vertical. The worst mailboxes were those that loyal mutt dogs felt obliged to guard.

All the boxes were on the north side of the road, presumably so the mailman could deliver the mail going only one direction and then hightail it back out of there, which is what he did. Who could blame him? The court reports in the county seat newspaper, in the biggest nearby town, regularly listed many of the addressees on RR 5. Mail was delivered – as far as could be ascertained from reading this paper – to rapists, child molesters, forgers, druggies, brawlers, murderers, and thieves of every variety. But to be fair, there were relatively few criminals, most of whom were diversified in the crimes they had committed, as well as being charged and convicted for crimes they did not commit – depending upon the demands of the electorate and the timing of the next election for prosecuting attorney and sheriff. It always helped a candidate's prospects to toss a Fraley or a Lang into the county lockup for six months. If they weren't guilty of the crime they'd been charged with, they were surely guilty of something else and everyone knew it – including the Fraleys and the Langs.

The district representative to the statehouse, a banker, a couple retired folks, and a handful of regular working class families received mail as well. In addition there were several would-be addresses where the residents felt no need to put up a mailbox. As nearly as the mailman could tell, about two-thirds of the people on the road regularly received government assistance, about three-fourths couldn't keep up with their bills, one or two had investments managed by financial companies, and only three or four recipients knew anyone out of state well enough to receive so much as a Christmas card. Nearly everyone had correspondence with a law firm for some reason or other. On the upside, as far as the mailman was concerned, almost no one subscribed to magazines, ordered books, or had come to the attention of charitable organizations in endless pursuit of donations.

For decades the neighborhood continued thus, until around the time of the second millennium, or thereabouts. The rural route system of road naming had long since been abandoned – and several road names had been tried – to the annoyance of longtime residents like Monroe and Goldie who suffered through a sequence of address-changing paperwork and mail snafus without moving even once.

The more notable change though was that folks started turning up dead in greater numbers than usual, even for that specific dead end road. It had always been the kind of place where death maintained a steady presence. Farming accidents, firearms accidents, violent domestic disputes, drug overdoses, and poor health care conspired with one another to create an ambivalent, even cavalier, perception of death. For instance, when Duke Clausen turned up dead, the official investigative report said he drowned in his bathtub. It omitted that he was kneeling outside it and that only his head and shirt were wet. The neighborhood was better off without him. The same could be said of Newt McBride who was found in the ash of his burned up house. It wasn't important that his skull had been penetrated by a rifle slug. The report listed the fire and omitted the bullet. It would have been fine if the killing had stopped there.

But it didn't.

There must be a murderer. Most neighbors fervently hoped there was only one murderer, and they hoped it wasn't someone they liked.

THE LAW IN THE COUNTY

EVERYONE ACCEPTED AS FACT that the law in Mac County was as useless, irrelevant, and ubiquitous as dog pecker gnats on mutts. Each of the three or four itty-bitty towns in the county had a patrol car and someone to drive it during the daytime hours. These cops generally worked part time to supplement money gained from other pursuits, and essentially paid their own wages by writing speeding tickets to out-of-towners. The fines were cheap, as such things go, expected, as such things come to be, and therefore, paid rather than fought. In general, the competency of these officers was very low because the pay was very low. No training was provided as the investment would be too high because the turnover was so high. In truth, it wasn't a terrible arrangement. The towns could count on a little extra income from the fines, the officers could count on a little extra income till they found something better, and whatever crimes might be committed were viewed as the county's problem, because the perpetrators lived outside city limits – like almost everyone else, most victims included.

That left the sheriff's department. Chubby-Bubby Barnham had been the sheriff for so long that only the old-timers could recollect his predecessor's name. He'd run on the majority party's ticket for two decades, generally garnering a hundred or so votes each election, which was more than enough for a win. The only people who voted against him were those who didn't recognize that Edward was his given name. When he finally convinced the county clerk to put Chubby-Bubby in parenthesis between his given name and his surname, no one even bothered to run against him. When folks came to see Chubby-Bubby as too much of a mouthful, he came to be known as CB, which, by the time Josie arrived in the county, was the identifier in parenthesis on the ballot.

CB believed in peace. His own. And that mostly worked. He was imperturbable, and some residents theorized this was due more to his energy level than cool headedness, but in the end it didn't matter. He'd seen shootouts between feuding neighbors and love triangle revenge killings. And there were a handful of bad seeds who had it coming but didn't see it coming. But there were never great numbers of any of these, and by the time there was a corpse, anything bad that might come of the situation already had, and nothing good could come of it no matter what happened next. CB knew this. Everyone knew this. CB was fine with it. Everyone else accepted it as life in Mac County.

It was with this mindset that CB investigated deaths and crime scenes. The questions weren't "Who did this, why, and can it be proved?" The questions were "Has the damage already been done, is it likely to happen again, and does anyone care?" In some ways it was a brilliant approach, even though unorthodox. It suited his department's budget, his own conscience and ambitions, and more often than not, served justice as well – or at least didn't do it a disservice.

Still, he felt a need to cater to more modern – that is outside – expectations, or the appearance thereof. So, he hired his deputies for this. Their primary responsibility, like their town cop counterparts, was to write speeding tickets. But they were also allowed to assume more glamorous tasks from time to time. They were at liberty to arrest drunks, druggies, thieves, and those prone to pick fights. These arrests nearly always resulted in the perpetrators sitting out a few months in the county lockup – not necessarily because they were guilty, but because they thought a plea deal was the easiest solution, and there was nothing going on in their lives that couldn't withstand their absence. Besides, even though the food was bad, it was regular, and someone brought it to them. Plus the jail was warmer in the winter and cooler in the summer than their other options.

CB looked for certain traits in those he hired as deputies. They had to look the part: clean shaven, nice haircut, good dental hygiene, full uniform – clean and pressed. These things were non-negotiables and they must be maintained without reprimand or reminder. He required that his deputies be polite. Also, he found it preferable if they were not inclined to swear, and instead threw a few well-known Bible phrases into their conversation – which, overall, he hoped they kept to a minimum. The less an officer talked, the better. He didn't care if, underneath their trim façade, they were dolts; and mostly they were.

Cecil Gravis was the ideal deputy in CB's mind. He had well developed habits of neatness; he was used to doing as he was told; he liked playing the part of law enforcement officer; he gave the appearance of doing investigative work; and best of all, he wasn't sufficiently intelligent to uncover criminal deeds or perpetrators. Plus, Cecil had completed a legal studies program and earned a certificate, which bolstered the type of appearance that CB was trying to foster.

Indeed, Cecil Gravis was the ideal person to place in charge of discovering why folks were turning up dead and who might be responsible for the deaths. CB's hopeful expectations were that Cecil would find neither.

JOSIE COMES HOME

MOSTLY WHEN PEOPLE LEFT MAC COUNTY, they never came back. For all its peculiarities, it was only a tiny place in the great big world, and very different from most of it. Either its residents had no desire for, or vision of, anything other or more; or they could see that nothing other or more would ever happen there. The former stayed. The latter left for good. Still, there were the occasional exceptions. Sometimes a person would leave, make a fortune, or suffer misfortune, by their own doings or the doings of others, and depending upon the case, come home to either show off or hide.

Josie was one of those exceptions who left young and returned on the downhill side of middle aged. At the time of the murders, she had been home long enough that her presence was no more remarkable than the dust and flint rock of the dead end road itself. In fact, she was unremarkable even when she first arrived, seeming, by the standards of the neighborhood, to be neither unduly affluent nor poverty stricken, to be neither hiding from the law for recent transgressions, nor avoiding the repercussions of prior transgressions. She was born and raised on this road, left to do, and to become, nothing special, and came back to do and be nothing special again. If there was more to her history than that, no one knew it.

It was clear, however, that if the murderer, or murderers, were ever discovered, it would probably be through Josie, because her home was the epicenter for all information circulating in the neighborhood. For ten years or so, all news, important or trivial, confidential or widely known, would sooner or later find voice at Josie's.

Josie was a weaver. That's how she arrived – several looms in tow – and all that occupied her. Every activity in which she engaged was related to that single occupation. She had sheep so she'd have wool for her weaving. She had herbs and plants so she'd have dyes for her wool. She wildcrafted for roots, shoots, berries so she could medicate her sheep as necessary and expand her dye pallet – and all for her weaving. Even her horseback riding and her companion dog seemed only to serve the purpose of providing diversions from her weaving – allowing her to engage in it more diligently when she was rested and relaxed. Indeed, most folks' only mental picture of Josie was of her weaving – and the mental picture of her thus was all they saw even when they were in the room with her! In truth, there was little more for her visitors to work with. She offered virtually nothing in the form of intimate – or even personal – interaction with them. They could not be blamed for their shallow understanding of Josie – which exactly equaled Josie's understanding of herself.

Weaving is a sensual activity, physical, visual, tactile, both stimulating and calming in its rhythm and beauty, the warp slowly advancing through the heddles and reed, accepting the loaded shuttle of weft beaten into place. For anything but plain weave and tabby – the province of students and beginners – concentration is required for complicated treadling sequences, and the mind of the weaver becomes absorbed with the dance of physical activity – as well as the emerging textile. That both her body and mind were so thoroughly, productively, and pleasantly occupied kept Josie sane and satisfied through the years.

In fact, in many ways, she had abandoned her mind and her heart long before she arrived in McDonald County, not trusting them to know even the most basic things – love things, life things, death things. She determined that it was best, safest, for her to limit her focus to immediate practicalities, and to choose practicalities that were most likely to require her complete attention. Thus, she felt her serenity, perhaps her very life, was owed in no small measure to her weaving.

She surmised that weaving must confer some of the same benefits on observers as it did on weavers themselves. Her neighbors would drop by, settle in, and sit for hours watching her weave. Whether they were speaking or not had little impact on Josie as it mostly escaped her notice. Or at least this was the case for nearly a decade.

It no doubt helped that her studio, which was also her main living area, was comfortable – woodstove-warm in winter, open-air breezy and sunlight soaked in spring and autumn, and gently shaded and cool in summer. The oak floor was nicely finished, but not highly polished; the windows were deep set, large and plentiful, but not sparkly clean; and there was nothing dainty, fragile, or breakable about – all of which served to provide an aura of easy comfort.

In addition to her looms, there was a pine bench rocker, a stuffed glider chair with a glider footstool, and an overstuffed chair and ottoman upholstered in fabric Josie had woven. There were woven rag rugs scattered about and large upended stumps for side tables. There was nothing on the walls because there was so little wall space, and the log construction was left as visible on the inside as it was on the outside. The logs themselves were not the polished orange uniformly smooth and consistently sized affairs that constitute the log houses currently being built by the well-heeled neighbors. Instead, they were the gray of a deeply clouded autumn afternoon, old oak trees cut, barked, notched, and swung into place with gin poles by her father long before she was born. Rendered weather tight by scrupulous maintenance of the chinking, it remained sturdy these long years due to the skill of her father and the scale of the material he had at hand, the logs varying in diameter from twelve to fifteen inches, and each long enough to lay corner to corner, the length or width of the house. Mighty trees of humble history, their daughters and granddaughters graced the property even yet, and had grown mighty in their own right.

Her kitchen was open to her studio, sparsely furnished with a small table and two chairs beneath a window that faced the sunrise. Her cabinetry consisted of open shelves at the top, and curtained shelves below. There was a cast iron farm sink, a modern stove and refrigerator, and the pungent smell of strong coffee that had so permeated the house that it smelt as if it were forever brewing in the old pot on the stove – and if it weren't actually brewing neighbors felt perfectly free to make a pot – as long as it was strong and black – which is how Josie drank it all day every day.

For Josie, the house was very much the incarnation of her parents. Monroe was present in these walls and floors – much in the same way as he was present to her as a child – strong, supportive, stable, but in a mostly subtle silent way. Goldie was present as a comfortable simplicity in the openness and ease of the kitchen. Perhaps the neighbors felt them, too, because there was simply no better place for miles around to sit, sip a cup of joe, and watch.

So, her neighbors came and sat and sipped and watched and talked. It was as if the words slipped out of them as easily as sighing exhales, as if there were no listener, as if they were mulling over their lives with all its puzzles, woes, and blessings for only themselves and God to hear. Sometimes Josie could hear, too, but mostly not, depending upon the current demands on her concentration made by the complexity of her weaving. Even when she did hear, she seldom commented. She greeted her neighbors briefly when they came – usually with a nod and a slight smile wished them well when they left, and nodded occasionally in the interim – if it seemed they needed it – as assurance that they were not alone.

Perhaps, for some, it was a confessional of sorts, or a chapel. These seemed always to come alone, apparently noting amongst themselves whether a car, wagon, or horse indicated the presence of another penitent. When the signal was missed, and there were simultaneous visitors, they would be cordial, talking around one another, trying to determine whether the first to arrive was so nearly done he should go, or whether the interrupter should acknowledge as much and say goodbye quickly. Others seemed to see conveyances in the driveway, three chairs, and a reasonably clean floor as vacancies to be filled with butts in overalls or jeans – as an occasion for a town square meeting, for sharing old jokes and new gossip, for speculation about the weather and the price of hogs.

Josie found the latter groups more tedious than the former individuals, which is the best evidence that she heard very little of what was said in either case. Words were seldom capable of drawing Josie's attention from her weaving. She was impervious to market reports, weather reports, whispers of who might be sleeping with whom, worries about bills and the price of gasoline, problems with teenagers, frustrations with work, trouble with the in-laws or the family vehicle, complaints about the inefficiencies of welfare offices, the overbearing or stupid ways of law enforcement, and discussions regarding the symptoms of the most recent flu-bug circulating through the neighborhood. These topics seemed never to be exhausted, only exhausting, and Josie never took part, even when doing a section of plain weave.

That is not to say she was never drawn as the words from her visitors flowed by. Raw grief, passionate loneliness, abject helplessness, strong currents of pain could pull her away from her weaving, though it would not have been possible for the speaker to know, immersed as they were in the tellings, and as subtle as Josie's signals were. Her weaving would slow, but not stop. Her lips would press together in a thin straight line, her eyes would narrow, her breathing would become more shallow, her shoulders would slump, all as she tried to shrink into herself, to hide her heart from wounds of others, fearing her own wounds might thereby be exposed and begin to bleed anew. Spent, her visitor would leave. Josie, soon after, would leave her weaving bench, retreat to her bedroom which no one had ever seen, and fail to sleep because of the throbbing in her head, which echoed exactly the beating of her heart.

Even secondhand, pain transmitted from one neighbor to the next, borne to her through a witness rather than the sufferer, was often more than she could bear. Perhaps it was because the effort to subdue her own pain left her with no resources to cope with the pain of others. Or, perhaps it was because her own life had so little of anything at all in it in terms of pleasure or pain. She was close to no one these days. She had no one to share with, no one interested in her joys, fears, losses – and in any case, she had little of these. She was, with regard to her own self, quite numb emotionally, and in fact, numbness, blindness, death was her aim for herself. And though she never articulated these goals to herself, she was mainly successful in the attainment of them.

The vicarious life was the only depth to her, which is to say that there was no depth at all. For Josie it was as she intended: the parade of life, its injustice and pain, presented to her a philosophical puzzle to be solved, and not much more. At least that's how she would have described it, had she been asked. It was for her a thinking problem, much more than a feeling problem, mostly because her feelings, if she'd ever had them to any pronounced degree, had long ago deserted her. There were two questions presented to her: Was there any way to make the world a better place? Was Josie living a life or hiding from one? She was acutely aware of the first question and completely oblivious to the second. In the end, they became inextricably linked.

For years Josie wove and listened. Or appeared to listen. It would be hard to say when or why she actually began to hear.

Josie Wove and Listened

IN HER TIME OF WEAVING AND LISTENING, Josie learned quite a lot about the little corner of the world called Mac County, and the dead end dirt road that was an even littler corner within it.

Having left McDonald County as a child – with the perceptions of a child – she hadn't really gained a sense of place. She had remembered the jagged flint, the red clay, the oaks and hickories, the clear fast-running creek that cut through her home place. But she had no notion of neighborhood, no conception of its people's personality, no idea of the lives that had fallen here, or never had risen from here. In the most non-religious of ways, she was born again as she sat and wove. It wasn't that she thought about what she heard, or compared it with what she'd experienced in her own adult life. Instead, it was an awareness that seeped into her as naturally and easily as the fragrant humid air she breathed. It was a remaking of self from the womb of home where the life she became and the life around her merged with one another. Having lost her life in Chicago, she had lost a sense of who she was there as well. Over time, Josie's very self would eventually come back to her – in Mac County – of the substance of Mac County.

For several weeks after Josie returned to her childhood home, she felt disoriented, as if she'd been dropped from an alien planet. First, and perhaps most unsettling, was the quiet. There weren't traffic noises – sirens, squalling tires, horns, or even the background hum of a hundred car motors. There weren't people noises – neighbors shouting to neighbors, motorists and pedestrians swearing at one another, no blaring radios. Instead, and only occasionally, she could make out the distant lowing or bleating of livestock in the distance, dogs barking, gun shots – apparently target shooting – and the wildlife – coyotes, bullfrogs, mourning doves, and crickets.

But if sound was mostly a vacuum, smells were a flood. Here, she could smell her neighbors' livestock and their businesses, if the winds blew them her way. Mostly, she could smell the day. She could smell gentle rain or oppressive heat. She could smell fallen leaves and mud and the melding of scents of a thousand plants.

The impact of the differences were so subtle and yet so pervasive that she found herself disoriented to the point of dizziness. And she struggled with the idea that she had abandoned Ty. She still wasn't clear in her mind whether she had come here to hide or to start anew and would eventually, after the murders, conclude that it was likely both.

Hiding, however, turned out to be impossible. Gabe showed up first.

"So, ya must be Monroe's and Goldie's young 'un. Ah knowed yer daddy and mama fer years. They's nice folks. Quiet though. Stayed to themse'ves. Till toward the end anyways. They needed he'p toward the end. Ah guess ya'd a knowed that. Er maybe not. 'Cuz, if ya'd knowed, ya'd a come… And ya di'n't come… Till now."

He paused, looking intently at Josie, trying to withhold judgment till he could size her up once and for all by her response. Sensing a vague tone of accusation, but not caring too much that it was there, she answered him directly without weighing words, feigning sentiment, or attempting nuance.

"I loved my folks and they loved me, but we weren't close. They never seemed to need anybody or anything except each other."

Thoroughly honest, though surprisingly brief, Josie's statement matched up with what Gabe understood of the Mansell's – and he judged her kindly. Gabe made such judgments only seldom and generally stood by them once he had. Many years would pass between this moment and the days of doubting whether he'd been right.

Josie judged Gabe to be an old man – perhaps as old as her mother might have been had she lived – perhaps as old as her father was when he died. Maybe this is what seemed to endow him with a parental quality for her; though the truth was that he was probably only ten or fifteen years older than Josie herself. He had a faint smell to him, perspiration gone rank, worn overalls, no shirt, ratty work boots, gray stubble on his chin and silver gray curls over his head.

He stood, smiled, waited, spat a stream of tobacco juice, shifted, sighed. Josie realized something was expected of her, but couldn't think what. It can be very slow going when the socially inept meet.

"Got anythin' ta drink?"

Josie was relieved at the helpful suggestion.

"I could make tea. Or lemonade. Or I've always got coffee."

"Coffee'd be nice."

Josie turned to the house with Gabe close at her heels. There didn't seem to be any way to ask him to wait outside, especially since he was already inside.

And a friendship was thus begun. Or, if not a friendship, at least a habit had been initiated. It was simply that nearly every day thereafter Josie would find Gabe through her door and sitting in a rocker, filled coffee cup in hand, before she had a chance to say good morning. He'd sit a spell, talk or not, depending on what news was being bandied about in the neighborhood, and then leave. Sometimes he'd return later in the day. Sometimes not. In Josie's mind, when she thought about it at all, her relationship with Gabe was not unlike being adopted by a stray dog.

Over time, and Josie could never recall how much time, from Gabe's telling, woven in and out of the visits of new, and then familiar, neighbors, she learned the stories that lived on this dead end road, occasionally funny, mostly sad, always without moral.

Over time, and Josie could never recall how much time, she found that she desperately needed a moral.

Over time, and Josie would know the exact moment in time, she learned she'd have to live without moral. Perhaps without even morals. And she would end her life unable to define for herself, in any clear or consistent way, what morals would have satisfied her, and whether morality itself was something she possessed, or thought worth possessing.

LILY'S STORY

SCATTERED THROUGHOUT THE FORESTS of southwestern Missouri, there are small open meadows rimmed round by a thick barricade of blackjack oaks and honey locust, admitting only quail, cottontails, coons, and small dirty children. The broomsedge grass and red cedar trees, that signal abandonment or neglect to adults, look like golden wheat and Christmas trees to children who do not consider monetary return. These are tiny sunlit places, secret and magical, excellent places for make-believe or reading. All children in McDonald County know such places and frequent them in their daily roaming, alone or in small groups, gathering nuts and berries along their routes, to enable a longer hunger-free stay. The Richards kids would often drag with them as they went pieces of scrap iron, old lumber, or various types of rubbish to serve as props for their play. Sometimes they'd bring puppies or kittens, perhaps one of the friendlier goats.

Adults are fond of thinking that the imaginations of children are unlimited, but it isn't so. Children build their make-believe on foundations they have been given. If they have never been exposed to fairy tales and picture books, their games do not involve castles or princesses. If they have never had a science class or been to a museum, there will not be dinosaurs or monsters, space ships or time travel. If they have not seen television or movies, there will not be detectives or cowboys or soldiers. The structures built by imagination might go to great heights and have fantastical features, but only if there is a place to begin building.

The Richards children had none of these experiences so their play was of a more practical nature. Mostly they built things: crude wagons and skids, halters and harnesses, chairs and tables, small animal traps.

Just getting out of the house was a relief, especially today. Their father Sam had his nieces and nephews staying with them because they had nowhere else to go. Sam's brother Quentin and his wife were going through a terrible divorce, terrible because Lily wanted it and Quentin didn't. It had gotten violent. For years Quentin had "slapped Lily when she needed it", and presumably, sometimes when she didn't. There was no denying it: Quentin had a temper and there were days, especially when he'd been drinking, that it didn't take much to set it off. The odd thing was that, for reasons unknown, Lily had begun to fight back.

Maybe it was just a timing thing. Quentin, annoyed about something trivial, kicked Lily in the ass as she was bent over filling the potbellied woodstove. Apparently without even thinking about it, she stood up, swung around and caught the left side of Quentin's face with a piece of stove wood. Quentin was so stunned by the pain and the sight of his own blood that he left the house. It's hard to know what Lily thought. At first she was probably at least as surprised as Quentin was. And then it might have dawned on her that she had avoided a beating, that maybe it was possible to avoid most beatings by administering them instead.

When Quentin returned home the next morning, somewhere between still drunk and hung over, his head about to explode, blood still oozing from a face going blue, he was in an ugly mood. He needed to reestablish his manhood before the whole household was confronted with a new and unknown way of being. It was territory he had no intention of exploring. Without a word he went straight to where Lily lay still abed and grabbed her by the shoulder. To his dismay, she rolled over with a hammer in her hand and got the other side of his face.

Maybe he should have waited till he was more healed, steadier, till his speed and reflexes had returned to more normal levels, maybe he'd even have to be completely sober, but he'd never had to make such considerations in the past. He had no experience with an opponent, only victims. This time when he stormed out of the house, he knocked over their few furnishings as he went, smashing as much as he could, but it was hard to focus on anything other than the pain. He was pretty sure she had broken his jaw this time.

It took Quentin several hours to realize that he couldn't eat because he couldn't chew, and for that matter, he couldn't even close his mouth in any kind of way that approached normal. He went to the hospital, they admitted him, wired him back together, and kept him a few days. It was during this time period that Lily saw just how pleasant life could be without him, how nice it was not to worry about what he might find annoying from one minute to the next, how quiet it was without him bellowing at the kids, in short, how good it was simply to be without him. To be without him emerged in her mind as the plan. She would divorce him. She told the kids, and the kids told their father when their Uncle Sam took them to visit. By the time

Quentin got out of the hospital, he was livid. What wasn't purple from bruising, went purple from pure rage.

Still, he had become a little afraid of Lily. Lily had always been afraid of Quentin and that had not changed. Not knowing what Quentin might do when he got out of the hospital, but fearing the worst, she took their kids – and Quentin's guns – to Sam's house – and the two room log house that wasn't really big enough for Sam, his wife and their eight kids, was made to expand for seven more kids.

Before breakfast was over, while the kids were still sitting outdoors – leaned against the wall, sitting on the boards that served as steps into the house, sitting on mattresses, and the few chairs around the table, eating cereal or toast – Quentin showed up. He did not greet his children. An aura of rage surrounded him as the smell of beer usually did, and the kids scattered, grabbing the littlest ones by the hand, some to the woods, a few to dilapidated outbuildings, and most of them to their special walled meadow of broomsedge and red cedar.

They sat and they listened. The littlest ones, who had been playing in the dirt yard around the house, had tiny metal cars and trucks with them, and made make-believe roads and bridges, hummed quiet motor sounds, and by all appearances forgot the fleeing and the reason for it. They had seen anger before and coped in their own way. The very youngest of the group, a girl called Stinky-poo by her older siblings and cousins, had brought a hand-me-down teddy bear and was pretending to be its mama. A couple of boys, eleven-year-old cousins, bickered about who had spilled whose cereal during their retreat, and it erupted into a fist fight. An older girl, whom everyone called Sis, the one who imagined herself in charge by virtue of being the senior Richards present, broke up the fight so she could better hear when the coast was clear for them to return to the house. She was the only one who sensed that maybe this time things were different, more serious.

It had been long enough for play in the meadow to approach normal. The cars and trucks were humming along through the grass, the teddy bear was being cuddled and rocked, and the fighters had turned their attention to trying to build a rabbit snare. Sis allowed herself to breathe normally and had stopped straining to listen.

When she heard sounds again, there was no need for straining or quiet, because the commotion had drawn close. Sam was shouting, "By God, ah ain't gonna have it! Ya ain't killin' Lily! Ah'll kill ya first, ya son-of-a-bitch!" Quentin was running toward their hideaway as fast as fear could take him, Sam in pursuit letting loose with shotgun blasts when he felt sufficiently close to hit. Quentin burst through to their clearing, enough slowed by the trees and brush that surrounded it, to allow Sam, who knew the area better, to catch up. Close and within his sights, Sam fired a blast that took Quentin's legs out from under him and stalked back to the house, assuming he had made his point.

And there Quentin lay. Surrounded by his children, nieces and nephews, hurting nearly everyplace it was possible to hurt, and in some places that hadn't occurred to him, looking up at the blue, blue sky, and thinking only of vengeance.

He called for the children to help him to his feet, but they fled, leaving him alone to think what to do.

What could he do? She'd hit him and then she'd outsmarted him. Lily had taken all his guns and ammo to Sam, and Sam wouldn't give them back. Lily had taken his pride and no one could give that back.

He couldn't abide that bitch anymore. He couldn't live this way.

He must have slept for awhile because it was nearly dark by the time he was able to get his legs to work well enough for him to make his way back to his pickup. He didn't speak to anyone as he passed through the yard and he didn't go into the house. He just left.

Quentin drove around for several hours, trying to think through his dilemma, slowing circulating through the dirt roads and possibilities. Finally, in the wee hours of the morning, it became clear to him that he had no place to go but home, and so he did. Making his way through the rubble of his yard, to his own shack, he came across his axe leaning against the wall next to the door. He took it in hand, took it in the house, and killed Lily deader than dead with it.

It might have been this story that awoke Josie's hearing. It might have been that Josie thought killing a spouse was justified in this situation, but that who did the killing and who was killed were backwards. Lord knows that's how most of the neighborhood viewed it. It might have been this story that first brought killing to mind for her. Josie herself would never know.

STINNETTS' STORY

THE STINNETT'S LIVED in an old tumbledown house rented from a California family who had inherited it from grandparents, never laid eyes on it, and had no interest in doing so. It leant up against the side of one of the steeper hills along the road, bare clapboard on the front side, a tiny window here and there, and a front door that didn't quite close all the way. Considering the neighborhood, they had an average amount of junk landscaping their place, a couple old vehicles, a horse drawn wagon, a scattering of rusted lawnmowers.

Snooks drew Social Security disability checks because of his emphysema. He couldn't even walk all the way around his pickup without leaning against it at least three times to rest and catch his breath. His wife, Maisie, worked long hours at one of the laying houses, grading and crating eggs. By the thousands. It was a minimum wage job (the owners could legally pay less), no benefits, and considered pretty decent employment for the area nonetheless. She worked seven day weeks for the extra money and had been there several years. She and Snooks had three sons together: a thief, a worker, and a "not quite right".

Josie supposed she should have remembered Snooks and Maisie because they had been around even when she was a little girl, but she didn't. Between the time she left and the time she returned, Snooks had succumbed to lung disease and Maisie had been worn by work to her grave. Josie was sure it wasn't so, but folks joked that Maisie worked right up till her last breath and died with her shovel beside her after digging her own grave. That left "the boys" as the tenants of their place.

The oldest Stinnett, Braxton, must have been behind Josie a few grades in school, but she could not recall him. He was a petty thief and a drunk, but he was neither industrious nor competent in either activity, and therefore had to resort to doing odd jobs here and there, mostly delivering livestock to the local sale barn or meat processor using his mama's horse trailer. In fact, it was only the sit-on-your-ass kinds of jobs that interested him, mostly errands for those whose cars had temporarily shot craps, transport for those who had appointments they couldn't miss – usually with a parole officer – and fetching grocery store items for folks grown too old to drive. When his income didn't come to enough to support his liquor habit, he'd steal something, get caught almost immediately, and spend some time in the county lockup. Often enough, he spent time in the county lockup for things someone else stole, but he figured it made up for the one or two times he'd actually gotten away with thievery. When his income, legitimate or otherwise, was enough to support his liquor habit, he had a tendency to pick fist fights, choosing only those opponents who were considerably smaller, older, or drunker than he was. In sum, Braxton was neither likeable nor repugnant, neither sociable nor a loner, neither trustworthy nor frightening. It was as if he were part of the scenery, like a twisted old oak tree, good for a tire swing, but carrying little in the way of real value.

The middle brother, Bennett, was the star of the family. He worked hard at a local feed mill, keeping the augers and conveyors running, and seemed to have a knack for doing whatever needed done. His weekends and evenings were spent doing the kinds of odd jobs around the neighborhood that required actual work, and often as not, a substantial amount of skill. He was able to do electrical and plumbing work, keeping old folks' tumbledown houses habitable far longer than the typical licensed contractor would believe possible. He liked it best if the old folks' paid him, but he took it in stride if they didn't, so he was often taken advantage of, even looked down upon by some. The common refrain in the neighborhood when something was broken was, "Get that dumb old Bennett to do it. He can do anything," and no one saw the irony of this. Altogether Bennett earned just enough money to keep Maisie a running and legal vehicle to drive, to occasionally go bail for Braxton, and to prevent the whole lot of them from sleeping in the rain, sitting in the dark, or eating out of garbage cans.

The youngest brother, Berke, was simple – as the vocabulary of the neighborhood put it. Maisie kept him clean; Braxton kept him in clothes and food. Rejected from the local school when he was less than a month into first grade, Berke never again left the boundaries of the dead end road, though he spent the entirety of every day, regardless of weather, wandering its length. He walked almost as if on tiptoe – unsteady, spasmodic – his height causing him to appear even more ungainly than he was. He always pushed a rusty lawnmower ahead of him, which afforded the dual benefits of keeping him more securely on his feet and also gave the illusion of purposefulness. Meeting neighbors along the road, or sometimes going into their yards if they were visibly about, he would ask if they might be interested in having him mow their lawns, and he would gesture towards his mower.

41

Depending upon the neighbor's time and inclination, he would be ignored entirely, in which case, he would wait expectantly for a few minutes and then leave – or engaged in friendly conversation about the weather, in which case, he would chat, pat the dogs, stroke the cats, and then leave – or he would be offered the job he mentioned, in which case, he'd push his mower randomly around the yard for a few minutes, request one dollar for his efforts, receive it and leave. No one expected actual mowing because his mowers were never started, as they mostly lacked an engine. Besides, Berke had no idea what mowing was, his own yard being carpeted over by decades of oak leaves and assorted useless junk. Even so, he had a handful of regulars on his route.

Bennett took him to the closest gas-station-bait-shop once every couple weeks, where Berke spent every single one of his dollars on Butterfinger candy bars. He ate all of them on the ride back home.

It was a sadness, though not one that attained to the level of grief, when Berke was found dead near his own driveway, tangled with his mower and unrecognizable, apparently having been dragged for several dozen yards. It was a tragedy, though not an unexpected one, when Braxton was found to be the drunken driver responsible.

Bennett, though he tried, lacked sufficient funds to keep Braxton from being "hit by the bitch", and sent to the state house for a long stretch as a habitual criminal, depriving McDonald County law enforcement of one of their usual suspects.

Josie could not remember how she learned Bennett's story, whether it had come to her by Gabe, as so many stories had, or whether it was in the air as background to dozens of other stories, or whether it was part of an explanation for why Bennett was hired by her contractor to do a lot of the work on the older parts of the house when she remodeled. Like so many other stories, it simply became something she knew, something melancholy in the way it seemed to trivialize life and death. Some folks said Berke was better off, and the folks who disagreed couldn't say why they did.

Here, in Mac County, on the dead end road that used to be RR#5, again and again, the stories were tales of death, sometimes violent, sometimes random, sometimes both.

Perhaps it was only the randomness that was the problem.

JUST MURDER

THEN THE RANDOMNESS SEEMED TO MELT AWAY, and the deceased were seen unanimously as vermin. Looking back, it might have been better had the deaths of Duke Clausen and Newt McBride been more closely examined. Maybe there should have been investigations. But no one cared they were dead, investigations cost money, the likelihood of a successful prosecution was low, and now it had become too late, at least according to the standards and level of forensic expertise at work in McDonald County. As for the deaths that came later, it would be hard even to make a definitive declaration of murder as the cause of death.

Besides, even the most law abiding and godliest of neighbors had to admit they'd like to shake hands with the man who killed Duke Clausen and thank him for his service. Same for the man who killed Newt McBride. Duke had been a predator of the worst sort, stalking the young girls of the neighborhood, telling them he was in love, talking about dating to them as if he were fifteen years old instead of forty-five, causing every conceivable kind of family rift in families that had more than enough trouble already. God knows he scored with a lot of these girls who knew only too late that he wasn't in love, they weren't dating, and he already had his next prey in his sights. Probably some daughter's father got him; and wasn't that a favor to every father around? A lot of folks looked at a bathtub drowning as a baptism, a cleansing, perhaps more intense than usual, but a good thing all round nonetheless.

And Newt? He was a bully who had swindled everyone for miles around, buying low and selling high from folks with few options. He'd swoop in at the first sign of trouble, look around for the few valuable possessions a household might own, offer a tenth of their value instead of a fair price to people whose needs were too desperate and urgent to search for other options. He'd snatched up antique cars, heirloom jewelry, hand raised livestock, tools, tack, and next year's hay crop, sometimes saying he'd be willing to sell it back when the sellers were on their feet again (a promise he never kept unless he could at least quintuple his money and sometimes not even then), and often foregoing such niceties because both parties to the transaction knew it was a farce.

Then he'd haul his booty to someplace where money flowed more freely, because there was more of it to flow, and receive ten times what he'd paid for any given article. His wallet, which he liked to show around the neighborhood, was so stuffed with one hundred dollar bills that sitting on it in his hip pocket had caused a permanent curve in his spine. Folks hoped the curvature was accompanied by excruciating pain, but doubted that it was. It seemed that sometimes even God favored those with fat wallets. Folks couldn't even speculate what sentimental heirloom or last hope Newt had made off with that finally caused his death. It could even have been a group effort that got him. Who knew? Who cared?

After all the visits and all the stories, after hearing about the deaths and the killings of so many, it was these murders, certainly premeditated, of Duke and Newt that must have finally penetrated Josie's abstraction completely. There was meaning if not moral, and perhaps there were both. Theirs were the stories Josie couldn't dismiss with a shrug, though it would have been hard for the tellers of it to notice her interest. Indeed, Josie herself found meaning in them only in her core, the part of herself she rarely acknowledged and never willingly visited.

ALICE COGGINS

IT WAS JOSIE'S NOSE THAT FIRST TOOK NOTICE of the Coggins.

Perhaps it was the strong smell that induced the profound sleepiness that engulfed the Coggins property, the only movement on the place being due to inanimate objects, mostly trash flapping in the sultry air. The smell was so strong it seemed colored – deep green, mottled brown, wavy, heavy, oppressively warm and sticky, impossible to move through or away from, rendering those who lived within it alien, contaminated, oddly inscrutable, unapproachable. It was impossible to imagine they ate, conversed, slept in those surroundings. Most folks assumed there must be stray dogs, feral cats, and outsized rodents on the place, but these were never actually seen. It was as if all entities, both living and dead were folded into the general category of stench and waste, and lay quietly within it.

Living in the very center of the septic refuse, heaps of shit-covered trash inching up to within feet of their bare bones bare board house, a house whose sides curved inward, itself repelled by the smell, or so it appeared, the Coggins family surely felt barred from escape.

Indeed, Old Man Coggins was the only one who left the place on a regular basis, taking his trash truck and his septic pumping truck on alternate days.

Most of his clients, after their first face-to-face, or more pertinently, nose-to-nose visit with him made arrangements to leave cash payment for him in a strategically placed empty coffee can, or in aluminum foil under a nearby rock, or behind a shovel in a garage, or in a feed barrel in a barn, or some such contrivance that eliminated the possibility of human contact. This suited Old Man Coggins very much because he was a busy man, not given to small talk. It suited his clients because they wished to avoid the surly old grunt and the aura he exuded.

Garbage hauled home from his rural trash route, Coggins dumped on his small acreage wherever he could most conveniently back up. Like a landfill where nothing was ever buried, bulldozed, moved, or managed, it was a collage of grotesque colors, smells, and movement enclosed by a fence papered solid with refuse. When he acquired his septic tank pumper truck, it was emptied in the same way. Even those most adamantly opposed to zoning laws, which the county did not have, were forced to reconsider their position during the hot humid months of August.

Old Man Coggins had lived in the neighborhood for as long as anyone could remember, and had seemed an old man all the while. No one knew his first name or wondered what it might be as it seemed irrational to consider that he was ever a newborn to have been given one. At some point in time, he had taken a wife, Ramah – a woman from a large family, all members of which would be referred to as developmentally delayed in today's vocabulary. A large, pasty glob of a woman, congenial and quiet, she had produced three children, one of whom survived. Unaccountably it seemed, this girl was of normal intelligence and striking appearance, although experts in this sort of thing would say that her normality indicated that the disabilities of her relatives were due to cultural deprivation rather than genetic abnormalities, and that her own intelligence had developed as sheer survival skill.

Unfortunately, the child, Alice, smelled just like her parents did, the only way a person raised in a landfill-sewage station could smell, and this prevented her from participation in any normal social interactions including schooling. Cleanliness might be next to godliness, but for Alice, it was next to impossible. They had no running water, no tub large enough for bathing, no towels, washcloths, clean clothing, brush, comb, toothbrush, nor any article associated with proper hygiene or attire. And this had been the case for so long that they did not miss these items or see the need to acquire them – even had that been permitted by Old Man Coggins – which it was not.

Old Man Coggins held despotic control of the finances, seeing the money as entirely his own – much as he saw his wife and daughter – and any expense unrelated to the maintenance of his vehicles was strictly forbidden. In fact, Coggins had tens of thousands of dollars, perhaps more, in cash hidden in various locations around his property, every cent of which was completely safe because no one had the olfactory fortitude to search for it. Coggins was a rich man. His family was destitute.

Josie had known the Coggins family since before she left for college. More specifically, she had known his wife Ramah, and her entire struggling family, when they were all children. While Josie had remained invisible and silent, Ramah, the youngest of her clan, was able only to be silent. She was the butt of jokes, the victim of bullies, a fat slow easy target. Josie remembered lunchtimes when food was thrown on Ramah who calmly wiped it away. She remembered recesses when Ramah was deliberately jostled, bumped, and pushed to the ground, into snow or mud or the brick wall of the school. There was never an effort to retaliate or any sign of rage. It was as if Ramah accepted her treatment as her lot in life in the same way one might accept a cowlick or rain. To her shame, Josie could not recall feeling anything at all about Ramah, neither pity nor disdain, accepting life as it came for Ramah. As Ramah did.

Only one of Ramah's several sisters, all of whom were treated identically at school, had any response other than acquiescence. Myrtle, the youngest, was a fighter. Evidently, all the fight that should have been distributed through the entire lot of them, fell concentrated into this single anomalous vessel. Finding herself surrounded by a group of classmates, each one jabbing her with fingers, books, lunch boxes, taunting her with insults, laughter, faces, and poses, one day Myrtle found she'd had quite enough. It was their last mistake with Myrtle.

Big for her age anyway, strong like an ox from her hard life, she took a swing at the kid nearest her, and just kept swinging. She laid the first two out flat and bleeding, the rest standing in shocked disbelief – which enabled her to take out one more, but he was knocked only to his knees and was able to stumble away when Myrtle took aim at the boy next to him. By now, most of the miscreants had gathered their wits about them and began to run. This is when they learned how lethal a three inch diameter flint rock could be when it was hurled by a girl who had never had other toys. Two more kids were flattened by rocks to the backs of their heads.

And that was the end of it.

A teacher appeared and then the principal, and finally, the school nurse. Parents were called and became outraged. Myrtle was expelled. No one cared. About a year later, Myrtle had a similar altercation with older individuals at the local Dairy Bar, and she was jailed. This became a cycle for Myrtle: fight, jail, release, fight, jail, until she died in a knife fight on the inside. And still, no one cared.

In contrast, Ramah was considered one of the good ones all her life, doing the right things, accepting whatever anyone said or did to her, marrying her only available choice, bearing three children, raising one – or rather, raising one till she was old enough to wander the neighborhood.

When Alice was old enough to escape Ramah's and Old Man Coggins' unfocused supervision, that is to say around nine or ten years old, she took to daily walking the dead end road from her house to the highway, and then back, from her house to the petered out washed out trail at the other end – until one day, from her back door through the bitter cold, Jewel Delevan called Alice by name into a kitchen where cookies and hot cocoa were currently being served.

It was a singular blessing, long in coming.

JACK AND JEWEL DELEVAN

THE HOLY CENTER OF THIS UNHOLY NEIGHBORHOOD was the Delevan place.

It sat far back from the road amongst a dense scattering of mature red oaks and hickories, rusted out cars, trucks, tractors, and an assortment of unnamable junk. A diverse collection of horses, cows, dogs, and kids wandered around and through this acreage that could not be described as forest, meadow, pasture, or junkyard, though it had every element of all of these. A long driveway, consisting of gullies, flint rock, and red clay blown dry and dusty during the inevitable summer droughts, led to a cluster of buildings once straight, fine, and stately, now reduced to sideways leaning dilapidation and decay. There was a big old two story farm house with a wraparound porch, a once magnificent old barn, plus a half dozen associated sheds once intended for chickens, machinery, and whatnot. A silo stood beside the barn marking time. It had long been without its roof and there were enough blocks missing from its circumference to allow a tree sufficient light and moisture to grow up through the roof and spread its limbs through the sides. Judging from the girth of this tree, it had been about two decades since anyone had found the time, resources, or motivation to engage in meaningful maintenance on the farm or its structures. Nevertheless, the scattered and untended beds of narcissus, iris, peonies, and lilacs gave the place an aura of pleasant restfulness and grace. All in all, it was one of those rare places on earth that managed to be both peaceful and boisterous.

Nearly everyone in the county had dealings or doings here at one time or another, and the owners were neither looked up to nor down upon by anyone, spared of judgment perhaps because no categories could be easily assigned. In some ways they were the bridge between the working folks trying to make it and the thieves, druggies, and welfare bums that never would. They got along with the cops and the ex-cons in exactly the same way – which was a vaguely wary, but mostly hearty, welcome. They took in strays, mostly people. Stray dogs were mostly shot.

It could not be said that Jack and Jewel Delevan were the heartbeat of the neighborhood, but it would be fair to say they could hear it and that they knew its pulse and personality. They had both grown up in this neighborhood.

Jack came from a household that might be described as normal in most of the country, but was sadly less common in these parts. He had had a father who worked for sufficient wages to pay for their modest home and semi-reliable vehicles, a mother who kept a clean home, clean kids, and decent food on the table, and siblings who mostly stayed on the right side of the law and followed in their parents' footsteps.

Jewel's circumstances had been different. Her mother was of unreliable temperament and health, a castoff who had learned no skills as a homemaker. Her first husband died under questionable circumstances when Jewel was very young, and her second husband was a long time coming. Between the two husbands, she and her children damn near starved to death. They knew hunger, cold, near-nakedness, and the most profound uncertainty in their state of affairs from one day to the next. Jewel was forever scarred by the needs she'd known as a child, and it was this that made her beautiful.

She remembered longing for what Jack had taken for granted, lowly as it was. Certain though she was that Jack's mother looked down upon her and her origins, in many ways she wanted to emulate the woman, the difference being that Jewel was driven by her scars whereas her mother-in-law had been driven by social expectations. She craved to make a clean warm home where the food was plentiful and where children laughed and played with one another.

It didn't come in the usual way. She and Jack were able to conceive but a single child and he did not live to see his first birthday. Months after he'd been buried, Jack commented to Jewel that grief wasn't a pain a person got over – it was a pain a person got used to. Jewel agreed. Nothing else was ever said between them about their son. Yet, they became more tolerant and tender toward one another, bearing one another's pain as well as their own. Their sweetnesses were never seen by others, or even suspected, as outwardly, Jack and Jewel could be very grumpy with one another. Only they knew it was more a manner of speaking than a signal of anything deep or ugly. Only they knew the depths of love each held for the other.

Still, they coped with their disappointment and loss in different ways. Jewel turned her caring energies toward every living thing in need. Jack became a pothead.

Though they were both hard workers, neither of them were cut out for a nine-to-five job, a "may-I-help-you" job, or any job that required familiarity with the operations of a time clock. That didn't leave many options for earning money.

Jewel would sit with old people or little kids when their normal care-givers were unable or unavailable; and she had a handful of regulars. Some of them paid well, some paid intermittently, some paid through barter, and some didn't pay at all. Jewel received whatever recompense came her way with the attitude that she'd been given a gift rather than payment. That is not to say she was a pushover. Old people and children alike were expected to do what they could for themselves with a minimum of whining, and outright disrespect was not tolerated. Within those boundaries however, she was willing to do almost anything for almost anybody.

By all appearances, Jack's main contribution to the household finances was his willow furniture business. Running counter to the impression given by his surroundings, his furniture revealed that Jack had an eye for beauty, a sensitivity to the graceful, an appreciation for nuance and subtlety in nature. Gathering materials from his own place, neighbors' woods, and roadside ditches, he fashioned chairs, tables, bed frames, and knick-knacks from grapevines, willow branches, oak logs, and walnut stumps. He had a flair for the whimsical and, once made, his designs became patterns for every other similarly inclined entrepreneur in Mac County and beyond. So, his one-of-a-kind creations became get-'em-anywhere articles almost overnight, thereby forcing him to drop his prices accordingly. This didn't seem to bother him. It couldn't be helped that folks had eyes and built what they found beautiful. It was a hand-me-down world. He copied what he saw in nature. Other folks copied him. What could be done?

Besides, he could rely upon his other, less obvious, sources of income. Over time, potheads, the stable ones, make connections, and opportunities for employment are offered. The first jobs are intermittent and comparatively risky. As time goes by, and reliable closed-mouth cool-headedness has been demonstrated, more lucrative and regular opportunities become available. The penalties, if caught, become progressively more ominous as well, but this is offset by the fewer number of interactions a person is required to have. So, Jack had worked himself into the position of warehouser, a middleman – the person between the main suppliers and a handful of dealers.

Pot, in very large quantities, coming up out of Mexico in any number of creative ways, would find its way to one of Jack's tumbledown outbuildings. At any given time, he would have around a thousand pounds hidden away. He had been involved early on in a couple gun wielding incidents, had proven his mettle, and was able to maintain this business with the maximum amount of calm possible for such enterprises. He knew only two or three men of higher rank in this business and dealt with them only infrequently. While they had had no misunderstandings, he wanted very much to keep it that way, and he was more comfortable when he didn't have direct dealings with them.

He carried a gun for all interactions associated with this business, whether his counterparts were above or below him in rank. Everyone knew everyone else was similarly armed, and everyone knew it wasn't just for show. Occasionally, Jack was offered an opportunity to move up in the business, but he declined. He wasn't clear in his own mind whether it was because he didn't need more money or couldn't tolerate more risk.

Sometimes Jack thought his responsibilities would be fewer if the number of bedrooms in his old

house were fewer. At this moment, he had two...
...what? ...tenants? ...free-loaders? ...charity cases?
...neighbors? ...friends? ...under his roof.

One was a young man just released from the
state pen. Locked up for an armed robbery that was
actually more of a drunken dare. He was trying very
hard to get his life in order; and he had managed just
last week to land a job, not a great job, but a steady one.
Jack expected him to be out on his own in a few weeks,
and he expected that he would make it.

There was also an old lady living in one of the
bedrooms waiting to die of liver failure. It didn't matter
that she'd poisoned her liver herself with years of
drinking. The point for Jewel was that she had no one
else, nowhere else, nothing else open to her if not for
Jewel and an extra bedroom. The old woman had a
daughter who managed to die of an overdose while in
court ordered drug rehab, and a son who was doing
time for grand theft. She was old, ugly, gripey, stinky,
and nearly helpless. Jewel took her to her medical
appointments, picked up her prescriptions, cooked her
meals, and kept her as clean as the old woman allowed.
She bought her treats and trinkets, and listened to all
her old stories – the fantastically unbelievable, the sadly
believable, and the dozens of repeats of each.

Jewel, it seemed, was simply incapable of
factoring money issues into her decisions, instead
assuming that it would somehow be made available
when need presented itself. On this dead end road,
need was forever presenting itself. It was Jewel who
invited Gabe into her home, along with other strays, so
they didn't spend holidays alone. It was Jewel who
made sure the Richards kids had school supplies when
they deigned to attend, and declined to judge them
when they didn't. It was Jewel who made the meal for
Berke Stinnett's funeral, whose heart was touched by
both Braxton's and Bennett's plight. It was Jewel who

saw to a great many things, both great and small, in the neighborhood. It was Jack who had to figure out how to pay.

And so it was.

Old Man Coggins didn't find it objectionable when Jewel visited his place to care for Ramah; and Ramah didn't find it objectionable when Jewel offered to take Alice in permanently.

Seated upon a stool, drinking hot cocoa and eating cookies, Alice had found home; and Jack found this arrangement to be the very best Jewel had ever made.

Extreme need and deep love had found one another.

JOSIE: A FARMER

IF ANYONE HAD EVER ASKED JOSIE what things interested her, and no one ever did, she would not have said animal husbandry or herbalism. No one ever asked her because the answers were so obvious. She would not have given those answers because those were not her interests. They were her core essences.

Soon after moving in, seeking Gabe's help in the way of advice and introductions, Josie hired Jack and Bennett to build a barn akin to what was built on Jack's own place a half century earlier. It was smaller and equipped with adequate lighting and electrical outlets, and designed with the same care and attention to detail as the house. They also rebuilt most of the old fence and created several small individual paddocks opening from different sides of the barn, using Osage orange trees from Josie's land to make fence posts – the type reputed to last for decades because they did.

Her original intention, if it could even be said that intention drove her, was to provide herself with the only companionship she'd known as a child. She had childish wishes: she wanted a horse and a dog. She was not particularly trained in evaluating the conformation of breeds of either species, but her eye for beauty, balance, and function led her to choose animals of only the very best quality. She brought both Selah and Solomon home within weeks of her own arrival. Selah was a three year old gelding, green broke as they say, meaning he still had much to learn, but was rideable and reinable under most circumstances. He was a blue roan, mostly black with a few gray and white hairs sprinkled evenly over his muscular frame. His color and his size came from his Percheron dam, his agility and refinement from his Morgan sire. He was, quite accidently from a breeding perspective, a wonderful specimen. He was level headed, willing, attentive, and responsive.

Solomon was an overgrown mutt, a Heinz-57, ancestral breeds impossible to decipher except to conclude that mostly they must have been big. He was black with a white spot on his chest, extremely large, surprisingly agile and quick, and affectionate without being pushy or demanding.

Josie would not have admitted it for all the world, not even to herself, given that intimacy was so unfamiliar to her, and holding that such depths of feeling seemed vaguely obscene; despite these she grew to love Selah and Solomon with a quietly vibrating intensity that exuded life and welcomed more of it.

By the year following her arrival in Mac County, it seemed reasonable to her that she should raise sheep so she could work up her own fiber for weaving. Further, if she were already caring for sheep, it was only sensible to raise her own chickens for meat and eggs; and moreover, it seemed prudent to have a couple milk goats for her own needs, and in the event she needed to hand raise orphaned lambs.

She had, through Monroe's genetics, been given the inclination toward self-sufficiency; these seeds of inclination, having been germinated, sprouted in all directions. After her livestock acquisitions, it felt to her that she had ignored the obvious in not already having a vegetable garden and this was rectified the very next spring. Over the next few seasons, she progressed from buying seedlings, to buying seeds, to saving her own seeds which she started in late February in the sunniest corner of her bedroom.

Her inventory of plants also expanded from vegetables to include edible flowers, and culinary, medicinal, and dye herbs – the cultivated herbs leading to a rekindled interest in the native herbs and wildcrafting as she had done with her father.

So, within a very few years, Josie had settled into a routine. She rose with the sun, drank coffee till she was rendered fully awake, foregoing breakfast, she went instead to tend to her morning chores. From there she went to her garden or to the woods, devoting as much time as was required by the tasks at hand for the given season. Indoors, early or late, as determined by what was necessary outside, Josie would have a simple hearty meal made mostly from what she had produced on her little farm and supplemented by beef and pork she purchased from Jack. The rest of her waking hours were devoted to her fiber art, broken only by a twilight ride over her acreage, through the forest, or along the road. Josie on Selah, Solomon following alongside, became such a common sight in the neighborhood that people stopped seeing it – in the same way people no longer see any of the markers that reliably define their days and years.

In this way, on this acreage, living with livestock and the seasons, it was true that Josie had found her place. It was not true that she had found her peace.

JOSIE: A LESSON IN SLAUGHTER

SURROUNDED BY LIFE, it seemed that Josie had none within her. She tended to life, but did not partake in it. It was as if her affairs were undertaken by her shadow, not herself. For the most part, she was rationally present but emotionally absent. The ebb and flow of seasons around her, the very pulse of life that pervaded her activities – births and deaths, plantings and yields – did not seem to touch her, let alone penetrate to her heart. She was not even sufficiently involved in her own life to be considered aloof from it. In short, Josie was neither aware of life nor living it.

Years she sat at her loom, not noticing her gradual acceptance as a neighbor, unaware that she was the prime confidant of Mac County's secrets, and as such considered a trusted, intimate, and invaluable friend. Her backdoor admitted every resident and judged none. It was not because she was tolerant or understanding or compassionate. It was simply that she did not care, and often enough, because she hadn't actually heard. Her absorption in her weaving rendered her silent and her silence was interpreted as profound empathy. Of this, too, she was completely unaware.

Josie tended to her own bodily needs as she did to her livestock. In terms of nutrition, she believed in the necessity of red meat, perceiving herself to be an omnivore, much akin to bears and pigs. Although she had purchased beef and pork from Jack in the past, he wanted to sell only sides of carcasses, and this was too much meat at one time for her to conveniently dispose of before it became freezer burned and unpalatable. This was true even when she shared liberally with Solomon which she was inclined to do. When she finally realized it, she was startled that it had taken her such a long time to do so. One of her own lambs would be ideal! Raised to around a hundred pounds and yielding about forty pounds of meat, a lamb would do nicely. She thought two lambs a year would supply all the red meat she and Solomon needed.

Acknowledging in her mind that even cave people knew how to slaughter, she was confident she could manage it. Yet she wanted to be humane and efficient. It took only an hour or so of research at the tiny library in Joplin for her to assure herself that this was something she could, and indeed should, do.

Although Josie sometimes had a certain fondness for one sheep or another, it was primarily due to the unique characteristics of the fiber it produced. Sheep inspire emotional attachment in very few people, and Josie certainly wasn't one of these.

In springtime, after lambing, Josie sheared her sheep. At this time, she selected lambs she would raise for her own consumption, also lambs she would retain for future breeding stock, and she sent the remaining lambs to market. It was early autumn when she sheared her flock again, saving the retained lambs' wool for special use – as it was softer than the wool adults produced, and separated out the two lambs intended for slaughter.

Josie had readied a small pen inside the barn for slaughter, cleaned the floor, made sure the lighting was adequate, and purchased a gambrel that she could hoist using a small electric winch.

And then she lost her nerve.

She didn't want to botch it. She didn't want anything to suffer. In her mind, dying was fine, but suffering couldn't be tolerated. It was that moment between life and death, that space of time during which a creature was robbed of its life's essence but before its life was ended, that interval that marked the transition from everything to nothing – it was this that Josie wanted to be as short as possible. She wanted no part of a death that wasn't certainly and absolutely exactly that: death. She had to be sure.

Her strong emotions about the slaughter surprised her, so accustomed had she grown to not feeling anything at all. Josie was unable to ignore them. She needed help. Where could she go for help? Jack. Everyone in the neighborhood, sooner or later, was at Jack and Jewel's door begging for help. Why should she be any different?

So it was arranged. When the days became consistently cool, Jack would let Josie know when he and Jewel were to slaughter so she could watch. Then, later, Jack would watch and guide Josie through her first slaughter.

Only a few brown and brittle oak leaves were left rattling on the trees when the Delevan's slaughter was done. It was a young steer. All of their animals were pets to some extent, so Jack was able to walk up to the animal, scratch it on its forehead, perhaps as farewell, place the muzzle of the pistol where he had scratched, and pull the trigger. The animal stood for a second or so, dropped to its knees, rolled to its side, and began to kick vigorously, its muscles unaware that its brain had died. The instant the animal hit the ground, Jack holstered his pistol and withdrew his sticking knife. Avoiding the flailing hooves as much as possible, Jack quickly made a deep long cut from beneath the steer's ear all the way round its neck. The blood poured out, the limbs calmed, and the animal laid back. The connection between blood-letting and relieved stillness was not lost on Josie. It seemed an instant within that stillness that the animal was transformed from living thing to sustenance for living things. It had gone, it seemed to Josie, from life to life-giving, and the transition period was blessedly swift.

All the rest was done at a more or less leisurely pace. Jack made a cut through each back leg, inserted his gambrel, threw a thick manila rope over the limb of a nearby oak, and using a block and tackle raised the carcass from the ground. Blood flow from the neck was less than a trickle by the time the hoisting was done. Using his skinning knife, he made cuts along the inside of each leg toward the main body and connected these four cuts with a single long incision on the belly that extended the length of the steer's body. Working slowly now, taking care not to puncture the abdomen, he removed the hide. Later in the day, it would be thrown into the creek that ran through Josie's place, weighted down with rocks, and left till the hair slipped, Later it would be cut into strips, thereby creating the rawhide lashing Jack used to make his willow and oak stick furniture.

The hide removed, Jack now cut through the abdominal wall, exposing the guts but being careful not to puncture any of them. Josie thought it a wondrous thing: stomachs, intestines, liver, kidneys, bladder – multicolored, coiled and compact – a splendid machinery of life. Jack loosened a few ligaments and the mass rolled forward and fell, expanding, into a wheelbarrow Jewel had brought to catch it. Using a hacksaw he split the carcass down the backbone top to bottom. Remembering Josie was present, Jack said she wouldn't need to split the carcass of a lamb unless she wanted to do so. Josie nodded. This was the only verbal communication they had had in the hour or so spent from pistol shot to beef.

Jewel laid a clean tarp in the bed of Jack's beat up old truck so the carcass could be lowered into it and hauled to the house where Jack's work ended and Jewel's began. Jewel did one half of the beef, patiently pointing out possible cuts of meat, and gratefully allowing Josie's help as she learned how to process meat by cutting the other half.

It had been an exhausting, and curiously unsettling, day for Josie; and she was glad her lambs would be so much smaller.

A few days later it came time for Jack to oversee Josie's slaughter. Josie had been sleepless the night before. She couldn't see herself pulling the trigger on her lambs. Besides, she had read that the skulls of sheep were much thicker than that of cattle and swine, and a frontal shot was not always successful. Early on Jack himself had expressed some reservations, but head shots were all he knew to do. Believing that Josie had no experience with firearms and had none in her possession, never having seen anything to make him think differently, he had offered to do this part for her and she had agreed.

She didn't like anything about it. It seemed cowardly and hypocritical of her to have someone else do the killing. Yet, she dreaded an inefficient kill, one that might take several shots. Over and over in her mind, Josie considered the possibilities.

By the time Jack arrived, she was firm in her decision about how they would proceed.

"Are we ready?" Jack asked meeting Josie at her screen door.

"I'm going to do a kosher kill."

"Up ta you."

"I'd still appreciate it if you'd watch in case things don't go right."

"Ah said ah'd hep."

In the barn, Josie easily herded the first lamb into the small pen. Once in, using a method common to all shepherds for handling sheep, she placed her left hand under the lamb's chin and pulled its head back and up, allowing her to steer it in a backwards gait. She maneuvered it into a corner, and still holding its head up, she pivoted to straddle it. Now facing the same direction as the lamb, looking through to sunlight in the doorway, still keeping its head up and back, she took a deep breath, and paused a moment for the lamb to calm. The lamb was quiet, alert, alive. Acknowledging all this somewhere inside her, and cherishing it, she then brought her knife from its scabbard. Quickly, strongly, Josie made a cut just below the lamb's chin and her own fingers, running nearly from ear to ear along its throat. Instantly, the blood pulsed forth. Josie swung her leg over the lamb to stand in front of it as it dropped to its knees and died. To her eye, it seemed a more peaceful death than the steer had gotten.

At that moment, something inside Josie exploded. Debris she couldn't identify was blown aside, opening inside her a space for light. And feeling. It was too much for her to understand, let alone express, had she felt need for expression, which she did not. From that day forward, for good or ill, Josie was a different person. It was as if, upon the spilling of the blood of the lamb, her own blood flowed once again within her veins.

She was only vaguely aware of Jack.

"Well, then. That there wuz as fine a kill as ah b'lieve ah've seen. Next time ah do a sheep, ah'll do it jes that a'way. An' ah think ya'll do jes fine from here on out."

Jack left as Josie was hoisting the lamb. Before today, he had neither liked nor disliked her, having reason for neither, and that was mostly unchanged. But on some level, he had a new respect for her. Even so, and much like Josie, he had neither the desire nor the ability to articulate his feelings.

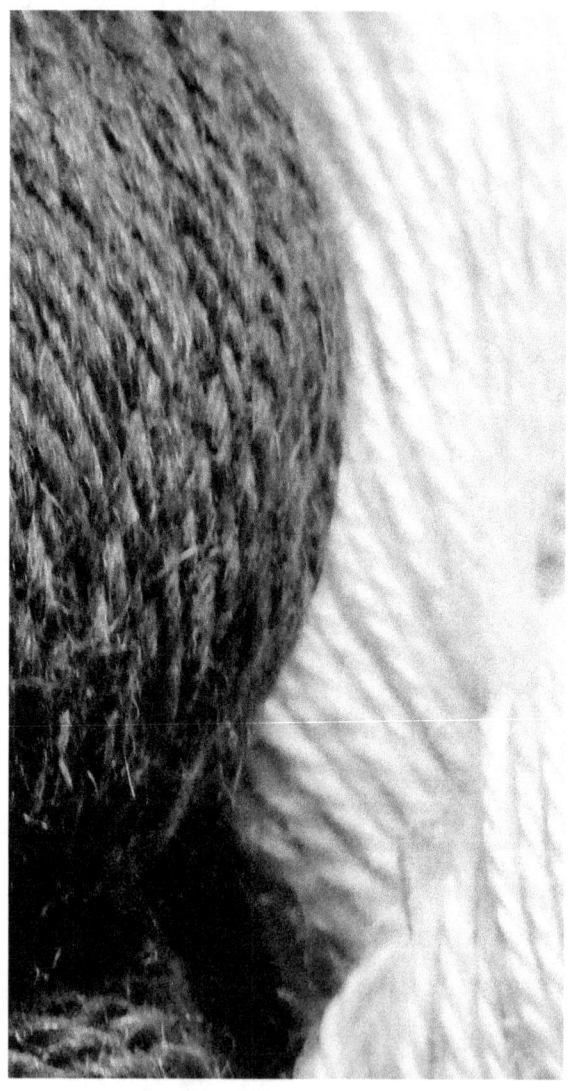

DYEING FOR BLOOD RED

JOSIE WANTED REDS for her weaving – reds of roses, reds of peonies, cardinals, and rooster combs. That deeply throbbing color of life is very difficult to reproduce in fibers. Madder plants can get a dyer close. There are other plants that give a promising bath, but no mordant can hold the color to the fiber. Most reds from natural sources are fugitive dyes, here and then gone, chased away by light or wear, washed away by water. Blues are hard, too; greens, not so much. Yellows of every conceivable shade are easy, held in dozens of flower species, both in blooms and leaves, as if the conceit of sunshine demanded it. Unless a person is in love with yellow, and Josie wasn't, other colors required more effort. Mushrooms and fungi held promise, nuts and bark. Roots, too.

She considered synthetic dyes as a lazy cheating way of producing colors, and – intense though they are – she considered the colors resulting from these chemicals as flat, flavorless, deprived of nuance, subtlety, and life. However strikingly bright they might be, she could only see them as artificial and alien.

Searching through the fields and woods, through plants and lichen covered rocks, seeing color all around her, the possibility of harvesting color never left her thoughts for long. A natural born scientist, she was not afraid to experiment, which always means not being afraid of failure. Josie tried acorns from red oaks, white oaks, blackjacks. She used hickory nuts and walnut hulls. She gathered mosses, alga, toadstools, and mushrooms. She planted indigo and madder, dyer's broom and coreopsis. She macerated, boiled, fermented. She tossed in rusty chain, copper wire, baking supplies.

Josie's efforts had produced an enviable palette of natural colors, but red, blood red, eluded her.

Her memory was so vague that the lesson might have been a dream. Monroe, with a tiny Josie at his side, pointed to a delicate snow white flower with but a single leaf at its base, both flower and leaf near to the ground, the ground covered yet with sodden oak leaves, too early for green grass or warm breezes. "Bloodroot," Monroe said pointing. Josie found it enchanting, the more so given that it was gone without a trace the next time she wandered the woods alone trying to seek it out – the plant a spring ephemeral, the color a fugitive.

As an adult, Josie researched it. The plant's name derived from the red latex produced by its roots, a dye used by Native Americans for face paint and baskets. Whether the roots had been used to dye wool, and how this might be accomplished, Josie could not find. The plants themselves she hoped to find again on her own place. Just barely too late this year, she would search next year when cool spring rains fell and then abated.

But, before then, in the autumn of the current year, Josie had discovered another way.

It was laundry time that turned out to be inspirational. Being adept at slaughter did not render it a tidy undertaking, and even though Josie was now able to do her lambs without Jack's help, blood was sometimes splattered farther than she expected, mostly by her own maneuverings, not by any suffering on the part of the lamb. The slaughter of her last lamb left her with several sizeable blood stains on one sleeve; and Josie was surprised at herself for how long it took her to realize this simple fact: stains are dyes! If it can't be washed out, so much the better! In all practicality, anything that could produce a stain, could produce a dye. Chocolate, wine, grass. Blood.

Blood stains. They were never the true red of cardinals and roses, but there was an essence to them, a hue, a hint, a depth that only life knows. She wondered if she could collect the blood somehow the next time she slaughtered – and from there, maybe, develop a method to render her wool blood red.

And so, in this, and in other ways besides, Josie became fascinated by blood. She knew that life was not possible without it.

And she also knew that, sometimes, life was not possible with it.

TIGER AND RUTH

"BY GOD, THA'S THE UGLIES' WOMAN ya'll ever see! They ain't one goddamn thing 'bout 'er face tha's right!"

It was Gabe and he was in fine form and full-fledged rant.

"Fer one thang, 'er nose ain't in the middle o' 'er face, it ain't a natur'l size, and she ain't got no teeth!" He paused, sensing he hadn't really gotten Josie's attention, which wasn't unusual, but this time he was vexed by it.

"Fer another thang, she cain't open her eye-winkers all the way no more, so's 'er whole wrinkly ole face droops down towards her chin. An' 'er chin's as crooked on 'er face as -er nose is – on'y t'other way!"

Still nothing but a nod from Josie and Gabe knew that meant nothing at all. He slammed his hat against the arm of the rocker.

"I swear to god, Josie, I don' know wha' it'd take ta git ya ta look up from yer weavin'!"

She liked Gabe, as she liked very few others in the neighborhood, maybe because he helped her be a part of the neighborhood, less adrift, more than a mote of dust in a sandstorm.

"Gabe, you know this is how I make my living. You know that if I didn't weave, I'd starve."

"Ya would not."

"Well, I couldn't eat and keep the lights on."

"It ain't the point an' ya know it."

Josie had no patience for this type of argument. "Okay. What were you saying? An ugly woman? Gabe, that's beneath you to berate someone's appearance. You've surprised me today."

"Wanna know why she's ugly?!"

"I don't want to hear that she's a sinner or deserves it or anything like that. It would change my whole opinion of you, Gabe."

"She's been beat ugly!"

Gabe was both triumphant in having Josie's attention and sick at the truth of what he was saying. He drew a breath to collect himself. Then he poured himself a cup of coffee.

"She use' ta be purty. Real purty. I remember when she was purty. Ah damn near di'n't know 'er when ah seen 'er yest'aday. Ah ain't seen 'er in years. She hardly ever goes out 'er front door. Ain't allowed ta, ah reckon. Ah wou'n't a-knowed 'er t'all 'cept she's with tha' worthless asshole she married."

And as such things go, now that Gabe had Josie's full attention – she had even turned on her weaving bench to face him – Gabe started talking to his boots. And he told the entire story to his boots. When he was finished, he and his boots left without even a second cup of coffee.

Ruth and Gabe had been schoolmates, though neither of them attended long enough to graduate. Playmates in elementary school, during recess and after school, they remained friends as adolescents, and had the serious coming-of-age conversations that young teens have. There were serious matters to be discussed. Neither of them saw the point of getting an education, and no one tried to convince them otherwise. By his folks' reckoning, it was high time for Gabe to be gainfully employed; and by her folks' reckoning, it was well-nigh time for Ruth to get married and start a family. Gabe was an only child, born to his parents late in life, much as Josie herself was. But his father wasn't healthy and they needed whatever income Gabe could procure, however small. Ruth's family was large, and they simply needed the space and one less mouth to feed. By the time they were sixteen, both Gabe and Ruth had met their destiny.

Drawn by the rumble of tractors and the rattle of brush hogs, bailers and the like, Gabe went to work at the local farm implement dealer, "Jay's Farm Supply and Service: New and Used Equipment". First charged with the weekly washing of the for-sale items, he soon learned the basic maintenance of lube jobs and tune-ups. Within two years, he was recognized as possessing a special knack with anything that had an engine, wheels, or moving parts. If Gabe couldn't make it run, no one could. Gabe thought of it as tinkering. Everyone else thought of it as genius.

It was a good job, as far as jobs went in that neck of the woods. The pay was decent, the hours flexible, the work interesting. Mostly folks were patient about waiting for repairs, and mostly his boss stayed in his office. It was his boss's son that proved to be the burr under Gabe's saddle.

Wearing his pricey boots and kicking dust, he'd wander his dad's business till he caught sight of Gabe.

"So, what piddly-ass thing you doin' today?"

"Well, this here Ford tractor of the Bullis's ain't runnin' right and ah was gonna see wha' ah could do 'bout that."

"Sounds like an important job. Real important. Bullis's piece of shit old tractor goes with their piece of shit Dodge pick-up, and that matches their piece of shit house. Important work. Have fun. I'm goin' to town."

Like that. Either the equipment Gabe worked on was junk, the owners were idiots, or Gabe was a sucker for spending his time on either. Gabe hated to see him coming.

Everyone called him Tiger because his daddy did, even though he was slight of build and cowardly in nature, until finally no one remembered what his real name was. "Jay's no good kid," was as close as anyone could come. Spoiled. Maybe because he didn't have a mama, his daddy saw to it he had the best of everything else: horses, cars, clothes, and girls.

Ruth was the best of everything to Gabe's way of thinking. She was sweet, a little bit shy, eager to please, beautiful in her bearing and her body. He guessed she deserved a rich kid husband like Tiger, someone who could give her more than the poverty she'd always known.

Tiger overwhelmed her. He bought her flowers! He gave her compliments. He wanted her "for all my own". She was charmed.

Jay bought the young couple a little house on a small acreage, and brought Tiger into the business, meaning Tiger now got a salary for doing nothing instead of toys and gifts for doing nothing. Tiger's and Ruth's marriage certainly looked like happily-ever-after from the outside.

Never trust how things look from the outside. Especially in Mac County.

It was shortly after his boy Tiger married that Jay tied a rope to a bright blue New Holland tractor – Jay was always partial to New Hollands. Next, he threw the other end of the rope through the steel roof trusses above the shop, caught that end as it dropped, and looped it several wraps around his neck. Then he took his seat on the tractor and set it in gear. The brand new tractor crashed through the back shop wall, travelled another hundred yards, flattened the fence between the lot and a pasture, and finally ran out of fuel out in the field. They found Jay crushed up against, and parts of him nearly through, the truss. Mercifully, the rope broke before he was completely beheaded or they would have had to bury him in pieces.

Rumor was that Jay had left a note for Tiger. No one knew for sure one way or the other. They did know for sure that he was left nothing else. Jay was tired, widowed, lonely, and broke – the last, contrary to appearances. The only thing actually paid for was the house he bought Tiger and Ruth, probably by a last load of mortgage on his business. Thank God Jay had put it in their names, or it would have been gone like everything else. New Holland came and got their tractors, the bank took the buildings, the inventory, and the pasture with the smashed fence.

The irony of it was that Gabe's life got better after Jay was gone – in about the same proportion that Tiger's had gotten worse. He was still the best mechanic in the county and people still knew it, only now Jay didn't get a cut of the repair bill. Best of all, Gabe could tell Tiger to go to hell – which he did when Tiger asked to partner with him a few months later. And that was the last Gabe had seen of either of him for years. Occasionally, he'd run into Tiger in the neighborhood, they'd nod if they didn't immediately recognize each other and ignore one another otherwise. He never saw Ruth at all, but that's the way it was with some women, homebodies, shy sweet ladies.

Gabe looked up from his boots and finished the story about his seeing Ruth in the passenger side of Tiger's beat up rusted out pickup. "An', goddamn it, the on'y thang ah ken think tha'd make a woman's nose hang crooked one way an' make her chin hang crooked t'other way an' tha'd droop her eyes an' make her teeth fall out is beatin's! Day in an' day out, jes gittin' the piss beat out'n of 'er 'cause his daddy cain't buy 'im stuff no more!"

Just before the screen door banged shut behind him, he said, "Ruth warn't beat to death! But she shor was beat ugly!"

Josie went back to her weaving, but the rhythm of it beat against the words, "Marriage is a sacred trust, marriage is a sacred trust, marriage is a sacred trust..."

Several weeks later, the chill of winter beginning to threaten, the ground covered brown with oak leaves still crunchy, Gabe was soaking in the warmth of the season's first woodstove fire, silently rocking and musing, his most common way of visiting with Josie. They had arrived at that comfortable state of friendship where they could be present to each other without conversation, the type of friendship born of honest understanding of one another, rather than shared values or world views, though there was a sprinkling of those, too.

He had been rocking thus for nearly an hour, the usual time he spent each day. Finally, he said, "'Member me tellin' ya 'bout Ruth? That ugly woman? An' Tiger, her asshole husband? 'Member?" Josie nodded, as she always did at the sound pitch of questioning. "Well, Tiger's dead. They found 'im all balled up and chopped ta pieces under his brush hog. Well, most of 'im. Some of 'im was dragged out behint it. 'Twas that Cecil kid whut tol' me. He had ta gather 'im up fer buryin'. An' he puked. Ah don' think Cecil liked his job much that day! Hear-tell it was a big ole mess. A big ole mess."

He must have imagined it, but Gabe thought he could feel Josie tense up a bit, but the feeling passed and he could see that she was still treadling and throwing her shuttle. He sighed.

"Does anyone care?" Josie asked.

"'Bout what?"

"About Tiger's death. Or the way he died."

"Well, I reckon Ruth cares. Ah went by ta see her. Ah don' know why. Somehow seemed the raght thang ta do. She cried an' cried. But she said nary a word other'n ta thank me fer droppin' by." Gabe paused.

"Ah don' think them tears was pure grief though. Matter-a-fac', ah don' know if they was any grief there 'tall. Mebbe ah'm wrong, but ah'm thinkin' them was tears of relief."

Gabe stood up, and as was his habit, he rinsed his coffee cup, topped off Josie's cup with fresh hot coffee, and without another word left for the day.

A nearly imperceptible smile adorned Josie's face for the remainder of the day.

Still, it made Josie queasy to think how much was pure dumb luck. It wasn't that she hadn't given it any thought at all. In fact, she had put a great deal of planning into it, but she realized now that she had left too much to chance.

After Gabe's rant about Tiger and Ruth, Josie had made going by their place part of her evening ride with Selah. She varied her route, as she had always done, but she made certain Tiger and Ruth were on it. Every evening. And she slowed enough to closely observe the doings there, instead of simply passing by as she had done in the past. She even rode a circle, a great swath of it through the woods that took in the back boundary of their place, which was conveniently near her own back boundaries, as so many places in the neighborhood were. At first, she had nothing in mind at all – no plan, no objective, no reason she could articulate. At first. Yet, it became an obsession.

There was very little to notice. She never saw Tiger wave or nod, and she never saw Ruth at all. The house had not been improved or altered in the forty years since Tiger and Ruth had come to live there. It was minimally maintained in order to withstand the whims of the weather, because Tiger never acquired a tolerance for discomfort. He did not wish to be cold, hot, hungry, tired, or bug eaten; but his ambition and energies didn't provide anything above those standards. It had been so long since the house had been painted that it was impossible to tell what color it once was. Heavy curtains, probably old blankets thrown over curtain rods, blocked all view of the inside of the house. For some reason, Josie imagined it tidy, but bare and dismal, which exactly described the acreage as well. There were no outbuildings, no fences, no gardens or flowers, no discernible place where a yard might begin or end and a woodlot or pasture might commence. Most of the place was wooded, though little more than sparsely so, the trees having been haphazardly cleared for firewood. From their stumps, the progeny prolifically sprang forth covering the entire place with oak, hickory, and walnut sprouts, the majority having main stems about the diameter of a man's thumb.

The brush had become a problem in Tiger's eyes, large enough to shelter coons, weasels, possums, and the like, and thick enough to make it difficult to walk through when he cut wood. It had been several years since he had brush-hogged the place and he guessed it was time.

It was easy for Josie to know this. The brush itself told much of the story, being of as nearly uniform height as wild things ever are. Also, Josie could hear Tiger banging around his old tractor and brush hog, cursing, stomping, throwing things, pushed to the limits of his minimal skills trying to get them to run. It took nearly a month before Josie heard the tractor awaken and another two weeks for the blades of the brush hog to spin. Of its own accord it seemed, a plan began to emerge in Josie's mind.

Tiger was finally able to begin brush hogging just after the last of the oak leaves fell. This made it the ideal time to clear brush because the small trunks and twigs would be brittle, rather than green, springy, and potentially impervious to old and poorly maintained brush hogs. Given the condition of his machinery – prone to breakdown – and his typical exertion limits – minimal – Josie figured it would take Tiger about a week to rid his place of brush.

She chose her evening almost at random. Indeed, it seemed the evening had chosen her. She loaded her .32 Colt, her father's gun, long out of style with gun enthusiasts, but pleasing in its comfortable grip and light weight. It rested and rode easily in the pocket of her overalls.

Selah was tense and spooky at first, perhaps sensing something in Josie, but he settled soon and the ride was a pleasant one. Josie dismounted and tied him just west of the boundary she shared with Tiger and walked a short distance till she could see Tiger driving his beat up old tractor slowly back and forth across his acreage. In undulating lines because of the trees, but nonetheless predictably parallel, he drove toward her and away, toward her and away. The sun was in his eyes as he approached her. That and his turned down straw cowboy hat, made it impossible for him to see her, camouflaged as she was by the brush and weeds on her own property.

She watched for nearly half an hour, mesmerized and determined, almost losing track of time, till she realized that Tiger was probably getting close to being done for the day. She waited for his approach and positioned herself directly in front of him. Anxious, she could not wait. She began a straight slow deliberate walk toward him, her pistol now in her right hand. She was within twenty-five feet before he noticed her. He looked up, startled, and stared at her just long enough to see her stop, raise her pistol, take careful aim, and squeeze the trigger.

Josie was a marksman. The slug hit exactly where she intended, the center of his forehead just above the bridge of his nose. This did not surprise her.

It did surprise her that he didn't fall immediately over backwards. She'd always heard that the force of a bullet would push its target backwards! Josie was astonished. Her mental pictures of what would happen and the reality of what did happen were a mismatch she didn't expect. She couldn't even tell if he was dead! She stood stone still as the tractor, brush hog, and driver advanced toward her. Finally, a slight bump – a rock? a stump? a hole? – jarred the tractor from its course. Tiger slumped to the side, then backward, then tumbled off the back of the tractor and under the brush hog.

Josie didn't investigate. Or need to. Swaths of Tiger were pulled alongside her by the still running tractor and brush hog. Blood, smeared over such a large area, didn't seem to be in great abundance. It was nothing like a slaughter where the blood is pooled in a single circle below the animals. She sighed, turned, walked calmly back to her horse, mounted and completed her ride. When she passed Tiger and Ruth's place going the opposite direction of her recent rides, she didn't even turn her head – missing what would have been her only chance to see Ruth who was peering out a front window wondering what she should do about Tiger's dinner – get it on the table or keep it warm. If she chose wrong, he'd be furious.

Instead, Josie was deep in thought, wondering why she had never considered the stopping force of various types of weapons. Being a good shot was one thing. Knowledge of your weapon's power was something else. It would be best to have both.

If she ever needed it.

HUXLEY EVERS

IT WAS ONE OF THE FEW PLACES on R.R. #5, and indeed, one of a scant minority in Mac County, that was meticulously well maintained. Rigorously clean and rigidly tidy, a stranger driving by could easily believe that the residence was inhabited by a small group of nuns. Or surgical nurses. Or a benign, yet energetic, obsessive. Neighbors knew better. Their impression was one of malignant oppression and violence. And money. But then, they knew the occupant.

Many an evening Josie had ridden by Huxley Evers' place. To her it seemed remarkable in its tidiness and understated affluence, but evidently Selah and Solomon perceived something unsettling there, as both animals sought the farthest side of the road and the greatest speed Josie would allow in passing by. She found this annoying, but generally forgot about it by the time she got back home. On one midsummer evening though, Selah so veered to the opposite side of the road that Josie was scraped bloody by blackberry brambles before she got him straightened out. To teach him he had nothing to fear, she did what most horsewomen do, which was to go back and forth over the same stretch of road until he could do so calmly. Whatever spooks he was seeing, he simply had to get used to. It was a fight every step of the way, an unusual state of affairs between them, eventually becoming a battle of wills. Josie was forced to the extreme of her horse handling abilities, and Selah was worked into a lather by his nerves and Josie's demands.

Huxley either heard the commotion or saw the cloud of stirred up dust on the road. It was the first time she'd seen him in person though she knew his name from the talk that circulated through her house when she was at her weaving.

Most people called him Huck. He was of average build. This surprised her because for some reason she had expected him to be a much larger man. His eyes, though shaded by heavy brows, were nonetheless intense, his lips a thin horizontal line; and his entire body, as nearly as Josie could tell, was covered with abundant curly black hair. He was clean shaven, perfectly erect in posture, and impeccably clean in his white oxford shirt and creased khaki pants. He had a definite aura about him of money and power, though both seemed to emanate from sources unknown and probably best left unnamed.

"Trouble with your horse?" he asked, a slight tone of amusement coming through.

Josie's words came out as little more than grunts, speaking through exertion and gritted teeth.

"No. He spooks here sometimes. He's got to get over it."

"I can help."

"No. Thank you. It has to be me. He has to do it for me."

"Whatever you say."

So, it was with Huck watching that Josie finally accepted the level of calm Selah was capable of, both of them worn to exhaustion. And with no further conversation, they left Evers' place behind them. Instead of passing by there again on her way home, she made a wide circle through the woods over the washed out wagon tracks at the dead end of the road and came up through the back of her own place.

The next morning, when Gabe commented about the scrapes on her arm, she told him what happened.

"Ya di'n't let 'im have at ole Selah, didja?!"

"No!"

Gabe sighed. "Good. Huck shun't have nuthin' ta do with animals. Ever."

Gabe sat down with his coffee and Josie commenced with her weaving. Apparently Gabe's mind had settled, but Josie's had not. After several minutes, she asked, "Why?"

"Why whut?"

"Why shouldn't Huxley Evers have anything to do with animals?"

"'Cause he ain't a natur'l person. He ain't got natur'l feelin's. Josie, he's a real rarity in this ole worl'. He ain't jes mean. He's evil. Stay away from 'im, Josie."

She had never heard Gabe sound so certain and commanding, and she didn't know if she resented it or not.

"Gabe, I'm not sure I like you trying to tell me what to do and who I can see."

"Ah'm jes sayin' he ain't normal an' he's dangerous! Ya do as ya see fit!"

Gabe dumped his coffee down the drain and left.

Josie couldn't remember having been so curious about a person. Huck seemed decent enough. Why in the world would Gabe, not to mention Selah and Solomon, have such an aversion to him? Feeling the curiosity rising within her, she became aware for the first time of changes, changes in herself, a heightened awareness of, not only life around her, but life within her. She was slowly evolving, becoming. Becoming what?

It was as if she were shaking something off – a deep sleep, a cocoon perhaps, a veil. Too long had the process taken. Her growing up years, aside from an abiding tenderness for her father, held nothing emotional at all. Those seeds lay upon the barren ground, unplanted, unsprouted, dormant till she met Ty.

Bloodroot. Josie was like bloodroot. Like blue cohosh, black cohosh, bethroot – the women's herbs. They are unlike seeds as most are known. They offer no clue to life, no bloom or leaf, through springtime and summer. If there is germination, if there is growth, it is only underground, it is only roots. Tiny things, tangled, threadlike, without sunshine or direction, they linger there below the surface, as if taking a long time to decide what to do and who they are. For Josie, Ty was the sunshine that called forth the first leaf and a tiny flower, an ephemeral springtime of passion and beauty. Delicate the life was, dying back into the soil before the full warmth of summer. Dying back to its roots once more. It is many years between seed and root harvest for women's herbs.

Is the dying back a true dying? Her mind wandered again toward Ty and she called it away from him. How can life be short and dying so long? Josie. Bloodroot. Blood. Ty…

Josie did not allow herself to ponder questions close to her, questions well beneath the surface and sunshine. She was not ready. She knew she couldn't answer them. Her evolution had not yet pushed her so far as that. By now, she had only a sense of home and a child's sense of justice. She had also a nagging intuition that somehow her answers, when they came, would be writ in pools of blood and that the first strokes had already been made.

Despite the fact that her emotions were not unlike those of a mostly quiet observant toddler, her mind was efficiently and keenly adult. Still, it took quite some time for Josie to put the pieces together about Huck. She also felt an inexplicable desire to keep her need to know a secret.

Bennet Stinnet claimed to have done work for Huck.

"Ya know tha' big buildin' at the back a 'is place? Well, it's an arena. Sorta. Gots bleachers all 'roun' on the inside an' a ring in the middle. Gots its own toilets, too. Huck needed someone ta wire in a bunch a big overhead lights an' ah dun it fer 'im. He bought all the tools an' ladders an' let me keep 'em an' he paid me good on top a that."

"Sounds like a nice man."

"He ain't a nice man, Miss Josie. Ah said he paid good. Them ain't necessarily the same thangs."

When Josie was a little girl, the land that now belonged to Huxley Evers had been owned by the Websters, and apparently, like Josie's parents, and unlike most other folks back then, they had managed to keep all their land together rather than sell off bits and pieces of it to survive. She supposed Huck was a grandson or a nephew or a distant cousin. And of course, she mused, there was always the off chance that he had simply purchased the land. In any case, it made no difference. The Websters had been dead and gone for years and the land belonged to Huck now.

In fact, Huck had been one of several distantly related heirs to the property, none of whom had actually seen it. Huck bought out their shares for a tiny sum, built a home, and moved in. No one knew what his career had been that allowed him to retire to Mac County as a relatively young and wealthy man. The house he built was very nice for the neighborhood, stopping just short of magnificent or ostentatious.

Far back from the house was the arena Bennet referred to, and behind that were two buildings, smaller than the arena, but still of sufficient proportions to house a great deal of... ...something. It was easy to tell the buildings held something that required frequent attention because the access to them was so well built, perfectly maintained, and often used. A small backhoe was parked under a lean-to beside one of the accessory buildings, and a compact tractor with a bucket and back blade was parked beside it. Most of this was known in the neighborhood or could be seen from the road. A great deal more was known, but little more could be seen from the vantage point of a passerby.

Josie, her curiosity getting the better of her, and her conversations at home having produced but little, had taken to going by Huck's place on most of her evening rides. Selah and Solomon had grown warily accustomed. Josie gleaned but little more in her observations: she learned what Huck drove – a club cab pickup that likely cost more than any house on the road with the exception of his own – and that, while he was home most of the time, his infrequent absences were usually lengthy ones, ordinarily a week or more.

Months of watching produced no more information until the first cold days of winter when Josie saw Old Man Coggins at Huck's! A more unlikely pair was impossible to imagine. Coggins pulled into the driveway just ahead of Josie nearing it from the opposite direction, so she was able to watch him drive past the house and all the way back to the accessory buildings with his nasty flatbed truck. He had something in the back, but Josie was too far to see what it might be, though she could tell that it was fairly large and mostly black. Clearly Coggins had done this many times as he didn't hesitate at the house or slow down at the arena. He knew where he was going and what he was doing because, apparently, he'd done it so many times before. Josie was startled to come to the only conclusion possible: Old Man Coggins had an ongoing relationship with Huck! No possibilities for its basis came to her mind. It was unfathomable. All she knew for sure, and she knew this only by what Coggins was driving, was that it had nothing to do with trash or sewage.

It was hard to be nonchalant, but Josie thought she managed it.

"I saw Old Man Coggins at Huck's place yesterday evening."

"Ah don' doubt it," said Gabe as he got up to throw another log on the fire.

Josie was flummoxed. She did not have elaborate social skills and was inept at subterfuge; and she was just far enough along to be aware of these deficiencies. She decided that if she could only move forward clumsily, then clumsily would have to do.

"Why? What could Coggins and Huck possibly have to do with one another?!"

"Jesus Christ, Josie! Do ya really think tha's yer bizness?!"

"Well, after all the gossip, rumor, and general neighborhood bullshit you've dragged in here over the years, I guess I did!"

And they stared at each other. It was almost a spat! It had never happened before and they each saw one another in a new light, but couldn't quite make out what it was they were seeing.

Gabe sat back down and rocked a bit.

"Ah 'spect ah was takin' out on you how much ah despise tha' bastard Huck."

He rocked back and forth another minute or so. Josie had resumed her weaving.

"Coggins brings 'im dead animals. Horses, cows. If'n sumbody has sumpin' 'at don' make it – an' a lot a stuff goes this time a year – an' it ain't fit fer people food – they call Coggins an' he'll haul it to Huck an' Huck'll pay 'im fer it. Sayin' it out loud don' make it seem so bad."

At this point, Josie wasn't sure she could agree, but she was still struggling with believing it.

"Ya could look at it as a service. An' ah guess 'tis. Mos' folks ain't got the means ta have their big ole dead stuff buried, an' it'd be a helluva job with on'y a shovel. An' no one want's ta leave som'thin big to rot – draws in critters. Firs' they eat the dead livestock an' when it's gone, they start in on the live livestock. An' Huck don' ask no questions 'bout how come som'thin's dead."

"So, Huck buries the animals…?"

"Sometimes ah think yer the dumbest woman ah ever knowed! No! He don' bury 'em! He feeds 'em!"

"He feeds dead animals?" Days later Josie would be able to see just how slow she'd been and that Gabe was perfectly right to be frustrated with her.

"Fer the love a God! No! Huck feeds the dead animals to live animals! An akchully, they ain't nuthin' wrong wi' tha' part of it!"

And with that, Gabe had had quite enough. He left Josie's comfortable rocker and warm fireside and slammed out into the cold winter afternoon.

She would have liked to have asked Gabe how Old Man Coggins managed to load horses and cows onto his flatbed, but once her head stopped spinning, she figured it out on her own. In pieces. It had to be done in pieces small enough for one or two men to lift.

But compared to what she had left to learn, this couldn't even be thought of as grisly.

HUCK'S BUSINESS

HUCK'S PLACE WAS A LONG WALK through the woods from Josie's, and she rarely took that direction. The hill between them was steep, crosscut with gullies, and overrun with blackberry brambles and every sort of brush. Besides, compared with most of her other neighbors, and the relative sizes of the properties involved, the shared boundary between Huck and Josie was short, only a couple hundred yards. Most of Huck's land laid farther south. Josie didn't know how much land he owned, but she suspected it was a tract at least as large as her own, and might have stretched southward far enough to run along the highway at its back border.

Winter, when a lot of the brush died back and the snakes were in hibernation, was the best time to traipse the wilderness between Josie and Huck. She couldn't help herself. It couldn't be done from the road because it would be too obvious if she just sat at the end of the driveway and stared down the length of it. Besides, the mystery of the place was held too far back from the road.

She chose a time when Huck was out of town. Her evening rides told her that for two nights in a row he'd been gone; and her past observations told her he'd likely be gone for at least three days more. After Gabe left that morning, she had a heartier breakfast than usual, and then locked Solomon in the barn so he couldn't follow her, giving him a giant lamb bone so he wouldn't resent it. She layered long handle underwear beneath her flannel shirt and overalls, put on her chore jacket and a stocking cap, dropped a loaded .22 pistol into her pocket, took up her hickory walking stick, and set out. She estimated that it would be about a two hour trudge each way, including some hard steep climbing, and that she'd need a couple hours to look around. It was about ten in the morning when she left, which would give her enough time to be back for her usual evening ride.

She wished she'd brought a watch. It was cloudy anyway and the gullies were so dark and overhung that it seemed later than it probably was. Her mood was more dismal than she expected, having lost her sense of excitement and adventure, she could feel only determination, and she didn't know what motivated that. Nor could she allow herself to think about it had she been so inclined. It was difficult to maintain her sense of direction and she feared a time or two that she might be lost, but she pushed on.

At what must have been the boundary between the two of them, Josie happened onto a two lane trail. The sun peeked out enough for her to get her bearings, and she realized this must be a seldom used right-of-way from the highway at the back of Huck's place through to his house. She was grateful to find it, the more so when she discovered it led all the way to the buildings behind Huck's place. This made the second half of her trek on Huck's side much easier to traverse, not to mention quicker.

The buildings were locked. Of course. How could she have been so shortsighted not to have considered this likelihood before setting out? In addition, by the sound of it, at least one of the buildings was protected from the inside by guard dogs. Josie was somewhat surprised by this, never having seen a dog outdoors and never before having been close enough to the buildings to hear them. Still, it did not seem terribly out of the ordinary.

After two or three circuits around each building, it was obvious to Josie that she wasn't going to find an easy way in. She would have to look more carefully. On the next pass, at the end of each building, Josie saw a small door, wide, but about half height, perhaps a clean-out of some sort, or storage, each secured by a simple cheap padlock. It didn't take the thought that Josie might have expected, and it made her wonder if she should have been a thief. She took the wire clasp from the right gallus of her overalls and bent it as nearly straight as she could manage. Sitting down, because she expected it to be a slow process, she began to twiddle the end of the wire into the key opening of the padlock. It surprised her that she was able to feel the tiny catches, but in the end it was only luck and patience that allowed her to spring the lock open. She raised the door to the first building, the one without barking dogs, and stepped inside.

The light was blinding at first and she shaded her eyes. When she could see, she found herself knee deep in moist chicken litter. Evidently the door was indeed a cleanout. Manure was pushed by the small tractor to this end of the building where it was loaded out. There was probably a pit or a pile somewhere on the place to dump it, and it was likely covered with lime to kill the smell. And then, Josie smiled grimly, after it had weathered, the mixture was likely spread on Huck's gloriously lush green lawn and fields. Well, good for him. No harm in that.

Then she looked around. There must have been fifty of them, all roosters, some of stunningly colorful plumage, others plainer and dull, each housed in its own individual cage. Josie couldn't comprehend it. What would a person do with fifty roosters? She could understand the pretty ones, the ones worthy perhaps of showing at the county and state fairs, but what of the others? Working her way from the pile of manure, and trying to shake it from her boots and pant legs, Josie made her way to the other end of the building. Behind an unlocked door beside the main entry, was a small room that contained feed and supplies. Bags of expensive poultry feed – and Josie knew its price because she bought feed of lesser quality for her hens – was stacked against one wall. Against another wall were lidded metal barrels. Josie opened one and jumped backward, partly because of the smell, but mostly because no one is ever prepared to see bloody hunks of hacked up dead things. Evidently Huck supplemented his high protein chicken feed with even higher protein raw, and somewhat rancid, meat.

The third wall of the small room was lined with kitchen cabinets complete with countertop, sink, microwave oven, and refrigerator. Opening doors and drawers, Josie found the cabinets, as well as the refrigerator, stocked with veterinary equipment and supplies. She also found a loaded pistol, similar to the one she was carrying, and a couple boxes of shells. One cabinet contained what appeared to be extensive records of individual birds, including blood lines, ages, and wins. A small box held what appeared to be cones of various sizes and diameters, most around an inch or so long. A razor blade, or some similar thing, protruded through the outside along the length of each cone. Josie immediately, and unwillingly, pictured it in her imagination. Spurs! These weren't just roosters! They were fighting cocks! The razors fit over their spurs to ensure that competitors would be sliced to pieces and the match end in a victory that left the opponent dead.

She continued her search. She had to see it through.

As luck would have it, her rummaging through the cabinets also produced a spare set of keys to the outbuildings, which she stole. She hoped they would be considered lost rather than stolen if Huck noticed they were missing. She was not worried about footprints or other clues because her steps would be hidden by fresh layers of muck long before Huck returned from his trip. The only other clue was the picked padlock – which she walked back around the building to refasten before she forgot. Then she let herself into the other building.

Not even the fighting cocks could have prepared her for what she saw.

The entry to the second building opened directly into another small room, similar to that at the side of the entrance into the first building. The cabinets, veterinary supplies, and such were nearly identical; but instead of barrels of feed and animal parts, there were safes, very likely filled with cash and records relating to it. Josie passed through this room very quickly, exiting into the main part of the building. Unlike the first building, it was dark and Josie searched along the wall for a light switch, and snapped it on. It must have been thirty dogs that instantly awakened to bark, growl, and snarl. Terrified for an instant, Josie leaned back against the wall to catch her breath. When she was able to focus and comprehend, she was both repulsed and mesmerized by what she saw.

Horizontal bars about six feet high formed a grid over one side of the main part of the building. Metal rings at regular intervals had been welded to them. To many of these, chains of meticulously measured length had been attached. Each chain extended to a dog's collar or a hook. Those that attached to a dog were of precisely such length that dogs could almost, but not quite, reach one another. Chunks of meat were hung from the hooks on the other chains. Gauging from the sizes of dead animal pieces Josie saw toward the back of the building – next to the cleanout piled with dog shit – when first hung, a piece of meat would be easily accessible to the dog for which it was intended. As the dog ate, however, the meat would become progressively more difficult to obtain, the dog would become increasingly hungry, and correspondingly more desperate. In some cases, the meat was left dangling between two dogs, who spent their time attempting to fight with one another over it, but just barely able to touch one another.

Water was available in bowls formed in the concrete flooring. Momentarily detached from the implications of what she saw, Josie thought this clever. A dog would never be able to tip over its water dish and they were shallow enough to be cleaned by a hose blast. In this way, Huck would be able to keep his dogs fed, by his own standards of acceptability, and watered for the duration of his absences.

Along the opposite side of the building were what could only be described as training stations. There were treadmills, weighing scales, handling equipment (extra collars, chains, break sticks, and so on), small cages for bait animals (smaller dogs, kittens, rabbits, and the like, plus mostly spent fighting cocks – anything that could begin, build, and hone a dog's killing ability), and pens with four sides and a top for the kill training sessions themselves.

It seemed to Josie that her mind was working in slow motion and that she was somehow outside herself and not really here, yet stuck and unable to leave. In this slow motion way, she remembered there was something odd about all the dogs. She turned to look, wondering if the strangeness was a visible something. It was. None of them had tails or ears, all having been cropped off as near the rump and as near the skull as possible. This would be an advantage in the fight ring, depriving an opponent of the ability to inflict easy injuries and holds. In addition, many dogs bore long jagged scars or had bits of their noses missing. In short, they were profoundly ugly – because they had been made so, not only in their appearance, but in the deformation of their very spirits.

Josie pondered this a moment. A deformation of spirit. How does this happen? There must be many ways. Is it possible to heal a deformation, or are they, by definition, permanent? What of her own spirit? And in that moment, Josie became aware that her own spirit might be a real thing, although she had no idea what its features might be, and she had no intention of searching to see it.

She shook herself back to her surroundings and panicked for a moment when she realized she didn't know how long she'd been gone. Immediately she made her way back to the door, locked it behind her, and began the trek back home. She felt no need to see the arena. She already imagined both it – and the doings it housed – all too clearly. It was likely a thing of genius as the other buildings were – exceptional in their efficiency though evil in their purpose.

It was a long walk home, and once she crossed over onto her own brushy ravine riddled property, the walk also became a tedious one. It was difficult to control her body and impossible to control her thoughts. What she had seen crept through her like a slow moving fire. Vicious avarice. Cock fights. Dog fights. Josie might have been emotionally underdeveloped, and she was certainly naïve in many ways, but she wasn't stupid. There must have been enormous sums of money passing through Huck's hands, a sizeable percentage of which he must undoubtedly claim for himself. He likely charged an admission that ran into the hundreds, if not thousands, of dollars. The bets probably ran into the tens of thousands of dollars; and he likely took cuts of that as well.

Huck had been careful to protect his enterprise. The access road from the highway at the back of his place provided a much safer ingress and egress to this type of event than a dead end road could afford. The buildings were ventilated to mitigate the smell; and they were nestled in the woods, mostly out of sight and well out of ear shot. It was a high class operation, so high class that reporting it would be dangerous. It would not be surprising if his clientele included powerful businessmen, crooked big city cops, and unscrupulous judges. In fact, it would be surprising if it didn't.

JOSIE LOOKS FOR JUSTICE

SHE THOUGHT HARD ABOUT IT. It's impossible to guess how many times luck might be a friend and she certainly didn't want to depend on it. In her own mind, she had been a sportsman, a marksman, someone skilled at scoring targets on a range. She had never thought of her guns as weapons and she could not imagine herself as a killer. Even after Tiger. There was very little inside her that made contact with what she had done, or what she was contemplating doing. She wasn't emotionally involved, at least in any way that pained her. She was not even cold. If she had thought about it, which she didn't, it would have seemed to her that she had no feelings whatsoever about the matter.

Rather, it seemed to be a philosophical question of how the world might be made a better place, and an intellectual puzzle as to how such an enterprise might be carried out. Josie engaged in the planning as she had in innumerable intellectual and academic exercises. She was interested, but not obsessed or stressed; careful, but not compulsive; aware of benefits and risks, but discounting the value of life for its own sake – and that including her own life. There did seem to be an annoying, persistent, and unaccountable obstruction that popped up in her thinking from time to time. Blood. It was the presence, abundance, absence, power, and meaning of blood. She could neither forget it nor find a way to calculate its impact on possible plans.

Simplest plans are the best. The fewer the details – the fewer the parts and pieces, so to speak – the fewer the possibilities for things to go wrong. In the end, she decided to just do it. Forget the planning, the thinking, the intrusion of blood upon her thoughts. Just do it.

Over the course of the past several months, since her first walk over to Huck's place in early winter, through till early spring, she had been back across the woods many times, had let herself into the buildings nearly every time he was out of town, had become familiar with the dogs, had learned to steel herself against the misery she witnessed. She also spied upon his place when he was home, crouching in the woods to observe his activities and routines. Knowing what he kept on the back of his place, and how he tended it, made it easier for her to decipher the little activity she witnessed when passing by the front of it on her rides along the dirt road.

In addition to Old Man Coggins, she would see a neighbor visit from time to time. Always they were men, and they never stayed long and there didn't seem to be any cheer associated with the encounters. Only rarely did she see a vehicle she didn't recognize, but when she did, she couldn't help but note how out-of-place they looked in the neighborhood for their luxuriousness.

Josie chose a day when Huck had just returned from one of his trips. In the very early morning, before sunup, with just barely enough light to make her way down a route still very overgrown, but now well known, she set out. Only this time she was armed with a weapon that slowed her progress a bit – a 12-gauge shotgun loaded with slugs. She knew she would arrive well before Huck's usual time to see to his animals. Although she didn't think it necessary to take any particular care to be quieter than usual – the dogs knew her step and scent, and she had never fed them, so they had no reason to bark to get her attention – she was aware that when she moved from behind the building to its front to let herself in, she would be visible from the house if Huck was positioned just right within it and happened to look out at the exact moment when she was exposed. Still, Josie reasoned that, statistically speaking, the odds for that misfortune were extremely low, and would present a complication to her plan rather than a total failure in its execution. Even so, she thought it best to minimize her time in front of the building, and quickened her pace when she reached its corner.

She attributed her success in letting herself into the building to good odds rather than blind luck, and, as such, not surprising. Once in, now very familiar with the building, she didn't need to turn on the light; and she walked down the center of the building to its opposite end, positioning herself just out of sight of the door behind the bait animal cages. According to her plan, she'd have to wait just under an hour for Huck to walk through the door. She couldn't be sure what his exact routing was once inside the building, but whatever it was, he'd have to be in the center aisle at least part of the time, and he would be walking toward her.

It was proof to her that it's impossible to take everything into account when planning something like this – that her presence stirred excitement and nervousness among the bait animals. While the dogs had become used to her, the bait animals, who were never around very long, did not have the same familiarity and calmness, especially when she was so close. Josie was glad that she had this small time cushion for them to settle a little before Huck's arrival.

It turned out that she needn't have worried. When Huck let himself in and turned on the lights, she saw that he was wearing shooter's muffs over his ears to block the noise of barking dogs, who awaited a feed time too long in coming. He wore dark navy coveralls that tucked into tall rubber boots, safety goggles, and leather gloves. In sum, his attire was such as to block his hearing, obstruct his vision, and inhibit his mobility – as well as keep him as clean as possible given the job at hand.

Josie watched him walk down the aisle toward her and the bait animals, evidently planning a practice kill session while his dogs were still desperately hungry. When he was about thirty feet distant, she pumped the shotgun to chamber a round, grateful that he couldn't hear it, raised from her crouch and pivoted to face him. She took aim at his abdomen just below the sternum. It took Huck a moment to register that there was someone in the building with him and another moment to register that he was in danger. It was a moment too long. Josie had pulled the trigger and hit where she intended. She was so near and the impact so powerful, that he was blown backward off his feet into a mist of his own blood and soft tissue. Even so, it took several seconds before he was completely still.

The dogs were instantly silenced by the sound of the blast, but as the shock wore off, began to bark again, bringing Josie's attention to them and away from Huck's corpse. She didn't know what to do. After seeing their misery the first time, she had decided she wouldn't allow herself to actually see it again until she had solved their problem. Now she saw them. Crossing the aisle, she began releasing dogs. It was a melee. Some dogs began instantly to fight with one another, others ran toward the meat stacked at the far end of the building, still others ran to the bait animals. It was too much for anyone to handle and Josie didn't try. She had done what she could. She wasn't naïve. Every animal in here would have to be destroyed, but at least they wouldn't be subjected to deprivation and violence for months or years on end. And just for today, they would not be hungry.

When she reached the door, she turned to look behind her. A half dozen dogs or so had begun to tear at the gaping wound in Huck's abdomen. Josie turned out the light, locked the door behind her and slowly walked home.

Gabe's Telling Of It

"WELL, IF YA'S A-WANTIN' TA GIT TA KNOW that ole Huxley Evers better, looks like ya missed yer chance."

Josie was dressing her loom for a new project and in the middle of tying up the treadles when Gabe came through the door. From her position under the loom, she was able to catch only about every other word, but she was glad Gabe wasn't able to see her face.

"Ah don' reckon ya even noticed all the hullaballoo down there, didja? Ah swear, Josie, yer jes an ole hermit."

Josie positioned herself to hear better and dallied with her tie-up so she could stay hidden under her loom.

"Yep. It's a goddamn big deal. Lots a goin's on with the sheriff an' all. Mebbe there'll be an investigation even."

Gabe bent over to see Josie, "Are ya even listenin? Ken ya hear me down there?!"

"Yes. I can hear you. I'm doing the tie-up. It takes a while and I don't want to stop in the middle. So, go ahead and tell me what's going on. But I have to tell you, Gabe, it would be a whole lot easier to follow your story if you'd tell it from the beginning." Josie hoped her voice didn't carry the sound of her pounding heart.

"Well, ya knowed I tole ya 'bout Huck. Ah said he were a no-count S.O.B. an' all 'at... ...er... mebbe ah didn't... Ah don' recollect."

Josie offered nothing to help Gabe decide which way to go, but he had settled in with his cup of coffee, and decided to fill in any blanks he might have left earlier.

"Huck uz a violent man, Josie, but the kin' whut never put hisse'f ta risk. No sir. He got 'is rocks off by watchin' others git bloodied an' tore apart. Them kin' is al'ees cowards an' bullies an' Huck weren't no diff'ernt."

Gabe stopped to wait for a nod or a grunt or some sign she was still listening. Josie offered an "um-hmmm", and Gabe continued.

"Them's the kin' whut al'ees gits it inna end. Sooner er later, the'r deeds ketch up with 'em."

Josie offered another "um-hmmm", this one with emphasis.

"Cecil says 'twas the worsest mess he ever seen. Ah don' reckin he's got much stomach fer his job anyway, but others sez so, too."

Gabe chuckled.

"Ah'll bet Cecil's still pukin' a month from now!"

Not a sound from Josie. Gabe thought to hell with it. He was just going to tell his story – because it was such a juicy one to tell – and whether or not Josie heard it was up to her – which was the usual way between them anyway. He finished up with hardly a break for breath as if he were practicing for the next telling of this story and wanted to get on toward that.

"Enyways. He's dead. All's they foun' of 'im was 'is head an' 'is hip bones an' a coupl-a joints. Dogs et the res' of 'im. Mos' of 'em's guessin' 'twas murder on account of a guy like Huck's got a lot a enemies. But they ain' 'nuff a ole Huck lef' ta even do an autopsy. Leas' tha's whut they're sayin'. An ah reckon tha's 'bout right. Ain't no one knows how long he was dead. Ain't nobudy in these parts care who kilt 'im enyway. Ah reckon a lot a folks is glad 'e's dead 'cause a bunch of 'em owed 'im money an' he was purty stric' 'bout gittin paid back – an' then some! Plus, ain' nobody in this county wantin' ta search through a ton a dog shit lookin' fer clues. Some folks even think i's funny that a man as prissy as 'at there Huck was to be found in shit-covered pieces. They say they weren't 'nuff a 'im lef' ta fill a bushel basket! An' some folks think i's on'y right that he was et by dogs he kep' damn near starved a good bit a the time. Ah don' know who foun' 'im. Hell, ah don' know enyone who'd miss em ta go a-lookin!"

Gabe chuckled and continued.

"Some's sayin' Huck had big ole safes whar he kep all the bettin' money an' all the money he borryed out an' was paid back, but if they was really thar – an' ah don' doubt but whut they was – they's gone now! 'Cordin' ta Cecil, there weren't no money nowheres ta be foun'."

He shook his head.

"So, ah guess tha' means all debts is cancelled. Ah 'spec' tha's good news fer a lot a folks."

He mused for a moment.

"Too bad this here thing di'n't happen in time ta save Tiger's ole man. Tiger weren't nuthin, but his ole man was someone ah liked an' 'twas unpaid debts whut made 'im kill hisse'f. Folks like Huck don' care 'bout nuthin' like 'at."

He sat for a couple minutes lost in his memories.

"Now, on'y thing lef' fer them ta do is put down all 'em ugly dogs and stringy ole cocks. Ain't nuthin worth savin'. Ah think they're lookin' for heirs now. Prob'ly folks somewhere a long ways off. County'll prob'ly try 'n' git some money off 'em fer cleanup an' whatnot. Ah wonder whut his place'll fetch when they sell it…"

Josie emerged from the underside of her loom in time to see Gabe's back as he rinsed his coffee cup. He turned, half-smiled at her, and left to go over Huck's demise with other neighbors. It was a high old time on the dead end road that day.

Apprehension

SOMETIMES SHE WONDERED what she'd do if she ever got caught. While she didn't think of what she was doing as murder, and knew there would be some folks who would consider what she was doing a service – akin to shooting rabid dogs – she suspected that much of the world would disagree, and that laws and courts and suchlike would be obliged to do something to make things right – which in her mind was exactly what Josie thought of herself as doing. So, she could understand the impulse and forgive their ignorance – not having seen the things she'd seen, and they being given more to rules than solutions.

But none of that really mattered, none of the who-kills-who-and-why stuff was the point of these particular mental wanderings. The point was this: what would she do if she was caught – or about to be caught. On some days, she thought she'd be just fine in jail. She envisioned reading her days to an end. Prisons had libraries, right? Inmates were free to read, right? Inmates could request books from any library, right? Well then, she'd be fine. There were thousands of books she'd not yet found time to read, but wanted to. The world was full of many things she'd never even thought to think about! She could take those things in hand via imagination and have a very full life behind bars. Big deal. A lifetime prison sentence would be very doable. Besides, statistically considered, she was well past the halfway mark of her life's years anyway.

But what if she got an aggressive cellmate? Or worse yet, a talkative one? What if she had two or three cellmates? What if they just would not shut up? What if they wouldn't leave her alone? She would see herself accosted and see herself simply living through it – till her cellmate-adversaries became bored with their efforts and finally came to regard her in much the same way they regarded the bars themselves – cold, immoveable, perennially present. Then she could go back to her original plan of reading her life away. Doable.

Or what if she was given the death penalty? There were already several bodies and if they could be laid to her at all, the premeditation aspect would be a foregone conclusion. Josie realized with a start that she didn't care! Or at least not very much. She couldn't imagine death as something important. She didn't worry too much about what, if anything, came next. Rationally, there were only two possibilities: either part of her "went on" and lived a different kind of life, or it did not – in which case, she'd never know it! Both cases seemed about equally peaceful to her and, after this realization, she thought about it very little.

Still, she'd prefer not to get caught. She'd loathe being a headline, loathe the loss of her privacy, loathe having her name known and bandied about. What if they looked into her past? What if they found Ty? He should be protected. Whether he knew he had the need or not.

And sunshine. What about sunshine? And the smell of rain? Chirping crickets. Rustling leaves. She'd miss all that. And it would be a grief. But she was quite sure she could handle it. It would be the same bloodless death that Ty lived. And somehow, there was comfort in that.

Josie took a deep breath, settled back into the rhythm of her weaving, swaying right and left as she threw her shuttle loaded with the deepest of red flowing over and under her warp.

REBA

JOSIE WAS GLAD HER BACK WAS TO THE DOOR when she was at her loom because visitors couldn't see her roll her eyes when they greeted her through her screen and then stepped into her kitchen. She didn't know Reba well and didn't want to know her better. What she did know was quite enough. Reba was, quite simply, a whore with aspirations of being a prostitute. In other words, she would have preferred to have been paid money for her services, but mostly accepted work around her house, or a few groceries, in trade. Any man of sufficient age or youth to get it up, and of sufficient horniness to overcome the inherent aesthetic limitations, had been served by Reba. This included men in the neighborhood and strangers dragged home from truck stops, bars, and the Greyhound bus station. Their stays ranged from thirty minutes – the time frame most common for the locals – to three weeks – the average tenancy for someone who hailed from parts unknown and farther afield. No one had ever hung on for as long as three months.

When Reba noticed that male neighbors frequented Josie's place, she regarded her as possible competition. She could not conceive of any relationship between a man and woman that wasn't sexual because she herself had never experienced such a thing. It did not occur to her that men occasionally desire nothing more than an open door, pleasant surroundings, a quiet listener, and a strong cup of coffee. In truth, these commodities, especially as a set, were surprisingly difficult to come by in the neighborhood.

The first time Reba banged through Josie's backdoor, she had fully expected to find every room in the house, except the bedroom, deserted; and she had planned to surprise Josie and Sonny in the act. The thought of disrupting young Sonny in acts only recently learned at her house made her sort of tingly with anticipation. Without knocking, she leapt into the house, and shouted, "Whut the hell's goin' on in here?!" For very different reasons, Reba's, Sonny's, and Josie's jaws all dropped opened. Reba was astonished to find Josie weaving and only absent mindedly aware of Sonny's presence as he yammered about the vicissitudes of owning an antique pickup as his only form of transportation (which presence in Josie's driveway had prompted Reba's house call). Sonny was embarrassed to have Reba in close proximity, given that he had only known her in her ramshackle house. Josie was angered by the rudeness of entry by a stranger.

Reba recovered first. "Ah'm sorry. That was a bad joke. Ah was tryin' ta su'prise Sonny. Mah name is Reba. Mah place adjoins yers over toward the south end of it." She said it well because it was actually true, and because if she'd ever had the capacity for embarrassment, she'd overcome it decades past.

Josie said, "I know who you are," and left it there. Josie's statement was also quite true. In the time since she'd arrived, having men around talking and laughing, it hadn't taken her long to learn who Reba was and how she made her way in the world. More details than that, she didn't care to know.

Sonny, who was rendered speechless for several minutes, finally mumbled something that must have been goodbye, and silently prayed his old pickup would start, because even if it wouldn't he was getting the hell out of there.

Reba, unperturbed, helped herself to a cup of coffee and sat down to watch Josie weave – while talking nonstop. Josie couldn't understand how the woman survived. She should have died for lack of oxygen because she didn't draw a breath through her entire monologue. Josie was aggravated to the point of anger – an emotion unusual to her – and couldn't think how to get rid of Reba. In the end, she reassured herself that Reba would leave when her jaws got so tired she could no longer speak. So she waited. In the meantime, Josie puzzled how Reba managed to bed so many men – hair dyed unbelievably black and permed to crinkly crispiness; a face both pock marked and wrinkled; scraggly, gapped, and blackened teeth exposed through chapped lips beset by cold sores.

After nearly two full hours of hearing Reba describe her life as that of a beautiful woman surrounded by countless suitors, after hearing her tell that bartenders wanted her to come sit at their bars so her attractiveness could lure in male customers, after hearing her stories of sadly having to tell one man after another that they were unsatisfactory and would have to leave, after hearing about the travails of motherhood unfairly visiting her too young and too often, after drinking an entire pot of coffee and brewing herself another, after convincing herself she had won a friend in Josie, she finally blessedly left.

Unfortunately, she'd come back from time to time. She was an infrequent visitor, usually prompted to stop in when she saw her most recent lay parked in Josie's driveway. All visitors would leave soon after her arrival and she'd settle in for another extended monologue. Josie had come to view her in much the same way as she regarded bad weather: unpleasant, unpredictable, seemingly interminable, but in reality ordinarily short lived. So, here she came again.

Dropping her fat ass into the comfiest rocker, newly made available, waiting for fresh coffee to brew, she started up. Josie tried to exclude the wheezing voice from her mind and concentrate on her weaving, but the treadling pattern was intricate and she had a hard time finding her focus. It was aggravating. Worse, Reba had deviated from her usual topic of male conquests and was talking about her children. Josie gave up on her weaving and tried spinning instead hoping she could manage the lesser required attentiveness. Reba didn't seem to notice.

"Ya ain't never had no kids, have ya? Well, ah'll tell ya they're a trial! They don' know shit an' they won' listen! Ah do mah level damnedest fer mah kids an' it ain't done one speck a good."

Reba had had six children. Her first two children were born when she was in her late teens by a man who was actually her husband. When he discovered she was cheating on him, he took his two kids and left. She never heard from any of them again and it didn't grieve her in any perceptible way. She was pregnant when he left and pregnant again shortly thereafter. The man who broke up her first marriage, according to Reba's account of events, left her for the same reason his predecessor had, but took only the youngest child, not being sure whether he or the predecessor had fathered the older one. This poor girl was left to Reba and was with her yet, now in her early teens. Two more children followed. It was anyone's guess as to who their fathers might be as the possibilities were so numerous.

These two youngest children, a boy and a girl, were removed from the home by social services several times, always for neglect, and had been placed in several different foster homes – some wonderful, some awful – as the luck of the draw for such things determined. Reba wasn't mean, or perhaps she didn't have the energy to catch a kid to administer a beating. Instead, she was lazy and selfish. She didn't know and didn't care where her children were, what they wore, or whether they had eaten. If they got sick, her only response was to hope it wasn't something contagious that might impede her own activities. It was a relief to her when social service would pick them up.

From time to time, she'd attend parenting classes, swear off her old ways, and do what was necessary to reclaim her children. Immediately upon their return, she would go to the county welfare office and claim Aid to Families with Dependent Children, her motherly instincts coinciding nicely with her times of greatest financial need – meaning if men were absent and it was not possible to extort from them grocery money or funds for the electric bill, kids were present. When men returned to Reba, the kids returned to foster care. Except the eldest daughter.

Her name was Clarice and by all accounts Reba kept her to do the dishes, the laundry, and whatever cleaning was absolutely crucial for survival. Why social services allowed her to stay was a bit of a question, but everyone supposed it was because she seemed old enough to see to herself, and the foster care system was overwhelmed even when only seriously abused kids were considered.

Occasionally Clarice would accompany her mama to Josie's house, but Josie couldn't recall her ever having spoken. She would nod or smile or accept a sweet tidbit to eat, but once this was consumed, or seeing none available, she would walk back home. She seemed sweet, both innocent and knowing, a strikingly pretty girl – tall and slim, blue eyes, dark hair, regular features – timid and alert, much like a newborn foal, striving for watchful invisibility.

The younger siblings, being away at some new foster home in the county, Reba was complaining about Clarice.

"T'ain't 'nuff no more fer a girl ta keep a house an' cook a meal. A girl's gotta please a man – an' ah don' mean in the kitchen! Ah mean in the bedroom! They's things a girl's gotta learn ta do!"

Josie felt herself getting queasy. Reba continued.

"Ah ain't talkin' 'bout love neither. Clarice needs ta fix herself up but ah cain't git 'er in'erested in normal thangs. She don' want no makeup. She don' want no permanent. She don' want no fancy clothes that men might find attractive. Ah guess she's jes happy wif 'er plain ole self. Ya seen 'er. Ya know whut ah'm talkin' 'bout. Plain as can be. She ain't got no more right ta Prince Charmin' than anyone. Stupid kid."

Reba sighed and paused, a rarity indicating her extreme consternation with her eldest. Josie was thinking how she might escape.

"Well. Jes t'other night ah decided ta take that little bitch in hand. Ah's tired, ya know? Do ya know that ole Luther Foster, lives on down the road? Well, he don' have no ole lady, but he got's his son, Leroy. Neither of 'em is lookers, if ya know whut I mean, an' Leroy's still got a mess a pimples even though he's gotta be nigh onta twen'y years old. Well, they both come callin' an' ah decided it was high time li'l miss fancy-pants Clarice got in on some a the hospital'ty! She usu'lly jes stays in t'other room, but she knows whut ah gotta do to keep things goin' 'roun' there! She acts like she's too good fer that sorta thing, but ah ain't gonna have it! She eats mah food and she sleeps under mah roof! She needs ta start bein' a growd-up woman an' he'p out!"

Past queasy now, Josie's stomach had really started to churn. She couldn't think what to do.

"Ah tole Luther t'weren't no reason his boy an' mah girl couldn't enjoy one another whilst me an' him was a'doin' it, an' he should go tell his boy so. An' I tole 'im tha' his boy shouldn't take no fer an answer! He's a big ole strappin' kid an' Clarice is tall, but she's got hardly any muscle to 'er. So's after me an' Luther got done, we could hear a ruckus in t'other bedroom, ya know, tusslin' aroun', an' Clarice yelled a couple times – an' Luther an' me, tried not ta laugh out loud 'bout that, but it shore was hard ta hold it in. Bes' we could tell, Leroy smacked 'er a time or two an' then got busy. It didn't take too long. Ya know how speedy young 'uns can be till they get the hang of it. Clarice's lucky ah di'n't do it t'other way 'roun'. That there ole Luther's got stayin' power. Clarice woulda been rubbed plumb raw. As it was, ah'm betting she only got her pussy wet. Anyways, soon's we heard Leroy slam the pickup door outdoors, Luther got up an' took 'im home."

Josie vomited.

Reba coasted to a stop: "Clarice ain't spoke ta me ner no one else since then... She ain't done the dishes... Er et..."

"Josie, ah'm leavin'! Looks like ya got some kinda real bad bug!"

Still on her knees, heaving so hard that it was probably yesterday's breakfast coming up, Josie couldn't even raise her head. Her whole house felt filthy, diseased, defiled. When she had recovered enough to stand, she immediately began to clean, starting with the vomit from her wood floors. She stripped wax, reapplied it, buffed it to a high gloss, emptied her kitchen cupboards and washed them and all their contents. She showered. She stripped her bed linens and replaced them, she stripped her unfinished weaving from the loom, took it outside and burned it. She showered again. Slowed by exhaustion now, she gradually wound the warp to re-dress her loom. In her mind a plan began to emerge from a haze of pain – the plan revealing itself piecemeal, disappearing, reforming, retreating, and finally presenting itself whole and clear. The world, or at least this corner of Mac County, would be a better place without the likes of Reba in it. And Josie thought she knew how to make that happen.

Since Josie killed Tiger and Huck, she had come to believe that her actions were motivated by her concern for her neighborhood, that she was making her small corner of the world a better place by exterminating its vermin. She had supposed someone else had done much the same by eliminating Duke and Newt. The killings of Lily and the Bennett boy were, quite simply, wrong. Did that not mean then, that some killings must necessarily be right? It was easy to find arguments to support her thinking. Was it not the same kind of thinking that allowed the death penalty and all war? Was it not the same kind of thinking behind much of civilization? Josie then, was furthering the cause of civilization by altruistic killing, was she not? It satisfied her to think so, when she thought about it, which she seldom did. She had grown to dislike thinking about it because her feelings had begun to rouse within her – and it was her feelings, she assumed, that held her morbid fascination with blood. Her next charitable murder, she resolved, would be bloodless.

BLOODLESS

JOSIE'S DELIBERATIONS regarding right and wrong, including all issues of judgment, were almost entirely confined to her training and career as a philosopher. Professionally, she had pondered systems of thought, ethics, ethos, and aberrations, as well as purely practical considerations.

She knew that for the most part, people learned their values from their parents and their culture, and it seemed to her that she had been failed in this regard. To Josie, it seemed her father walked through the world with a kind of peaceful neutrality, apparently unable to distinguish between good and evil, or else not seeing it as his right to judge, or perhaps not thinking it an important matter in any case. Josie had no idea what her mother thought about anything. Josie could not envision her parents anyplace other than here, and therefore, it did not occur to her that they possessed a peace born of experienced wisdom, rather than a naivety born of isolation. Oddly, given her education in philosophy, Josie never considered the culture of Mac County, even as her immersion in it was renewed.

In her faraway other life, the life of the professoriate and philosophy, Socrates always assumed the face and features of her father in Josie's imagination. Perhaps it was their shared association with hemlock – both men knowing the power of a simple plant, yet bearing no hard feelings toward it.

Chert, flint, limestone. Meadowlarks, hawks, kingfisher. Pokeweed, pigweed, wild parsnip. Hemlock. When Josie was just a little girl, she would walk out into the woods with her father. He would point to stones and birds and plants and introduce them to Josie, explaining that every single one of them was just being its natural self, and bore neither goodwill nor ill will toward any other thing. Monroe was careful to point out the subtle differences among wild parsnip, queen anne's lace, and hemlock. Mistakes were easy to make and hemlock was deadly. Monroe said that poisonous plants were such only to protect themselves and their offspring from predation and extinction, and by those lights, hemlock had done very well for itself.

Hemlock grew in abundance near the little spring that ran through the Mansell place and it grew there yet, its protective devices evidently having served it well. Josie walked to the far end of her place, not wanting to take a chance on exposing her horse to possible poisoning from poor grazing choices. Her plan was simple, though very different from the methods she used in the past, organic rather than metallic, cleaner it seemed to her.

Reba spoke often of the gifts men bestowed upon her. Catering mostly to the financially insolvent as she did, she preferred to give the impression that these things were more a tribute to her beauty than a payment for services rendered. A higher than average number of pot heads lived in the neighborhood – users, growers, dealers – so weed was often the medium of trade.

Reba was no connoisseur and she wasn't a specialist. She figured she'd smoked everything from premium bud to cow dung to pesticide laden – and all, apparently, without ill effects. She'd dabble occasionally in pills and powders, but meth scared her because she thought it made people ugly; and she was unwilling to risk her appearance, thinking as she did that it was her stock and trade.

Surveying the site, Josie chose an area that didn't require her to get wet beyond ankle level on her rubber boots. She stood for a moment and considered the beauty of the plant, recalling its appearance through the seasons, and appreciating how long it had been here – before her childhood, before her father's childhood, way back into the long ago, when natives would have known and respected its purpose and its power. She smiled, took a deep breath, and started to work.

Josie wore her work gloves to harvest a large clump of hemlock, using a trowel to insure she got a good chunk of root – this and the sap being the deadliest parts of the plant. It was familiar work to Josie. She often harvested plant materials for dyeing her wool so she was not the least bit concerned if someone saw her doing this. Even so, that event would be unlikely as far back in the woods as she had come. Besides, and this never failed to astonish Josie, she knew of no one else in the neighborhood who had even the slightest awareness of the marvels that grew all around them. Either they were too busy just trying to survive, had never been taught, or simply didn't care. Usually it was all three.

She gathered the stalks into a bundle, tied them with a scrap of rug warp, and walked home. She carried them root bulb down, trying not to lose the sap from the hollow stems. They smelled of a fresh vegetable sweetness, clean, green. When she got home, she went to her dye studio and loosed the ties around the plants. Working carefully, she cut away the roots, saving them in a large jar. Then she drained the sap from the plants into a smaller jar. She rarely had any idea what chemicals might be contained in any given plant, and thought more often in terms of shy plant spirits rather than in terms of science. Therefore, believing that tender treatment of the plant would give the best results, she protected both sap and roots from strong sunlight so she wouldn't have to worry about them while she was doing her evening chores.

After dark, she retrieved some premium bud – kush she had purchased in Chicago when she last visited her sister-in-law – placed it in a jar, added several drops of hemlock sap, shaved in a small amount of ground hemlock root for good measure, and sealed the jar to allow the sap to dissipate throughout the plant matter, figuring that overnight would likely be sufficient for that purpose. Josie enjoyed working with plants. There was a calm satisfaction about it, a oneness with the green world – and the larger world as well. The work helped calm and clear her mind as she focused on retaining the essence of the plant, its ultimate purpose far removed from her thoughts.

Early the next morning, she reopened the jar and used her hand to waft the smell to her nose. Sweet. Green. Both calming and exhilarating. Josie transferred the toxic kush to a bag, put it in a tin that once held Christmas cookies, and waited for her next visit from Reba. Only this time, she hoped it would be soon.

Her hopes were not disappointed. The day after Josie finished her herbal preparation, and about three weeks after her last visit, Reba banged through Josie's back door, this time causing Jack and Gabe to leave. She immediately dropped into her usual routine – pouring herself a cup of coffee, plopping her ass in a chair, getting her jaws going on useless chatter. Josie pretended to weave, knowing she would have to undo most of her work because of her inability to concentrate. No matter.

About the time she expected Reba to be wound down, she turned on her bench to face her, an occurrence so unusual that Reba stopped talking in mid-sentence, her mouth still open.

"Reba, I'd like to apologize for the last time you were here. I should have warned you that I thought I might be coming down with something. I'm sorry you had to be here when I was so sick!"

"Uh…"

"You've been such a nice neighbor to me and you're about the only woman I ever see. And men don't show the same kind of interest in me that they do in you."

"Mebbe if ya tried fixing yerself up, dyed the gray outta yer hair, got a perm'nent or sumpin. Mebbe if ya let 'em know yer up fer a tumble. Made the firs' move. Ya know?"

Josie was a bit taken aback at her interest, but then Reba rethought her advice, worried about possible competition, and changed tack.

"Well. But ya seem ta be doin' jes fine as ya are."

This allowed Josie to continue.

"Anyway, I think you and I are pretty close and I feel bad about last time, so I'd like to make it up to you. I want to give you a special present."

Reba broke into a smile stretching her cracked lips and exposing her black scraggly teeth. Rarely did the topic of gift giving come up in broad daylight while she was fully clothed and in a sitting position. And never with a woman. She was genuinely pleased.

"Come with me," and Josie motioned Reba to follow her into the room in her house that served as her dye studio. She presented Reba with the tin.

"I think you told me you smoke."

"Yeah!" Reba was investigating the contents of the tin, but her burnt up senses, on top of her congenital nearsightedness, didn't allow her to draw any useful information from her efforts. But she knew weed when she saw it and she knew she'd been gifted with some.

Josie explained that this was special pot that she picked up when she had to visit Chicago on business. Reba was taken. Big city weed! That had to be special!

"Well, ah thank 'ee!" said Reba, now in a hurry to leave.

"I think you should save it for a treat just for you," said Josie.

"Yeah, ah will – if ah ken keep that damn Clarice from findin' it!" And Reba slammed out the door.

Josie fainted.

Reba didn't notice.

CONSIDERATION OF CONFESSION

SHE WAS JUST COMING TO when Gabe saw her through the screen door.

"Josie!" Gabe rushed in and helped her sit up.

"Wha's a matter with ya?!"

"I'm okay. I'm…"

Josie's head was spinning. What had she done?! It had never occurred to her that someone other than Reba might be injured. She wasn't even absolutely sure what her concoction might do. She had no idea what dosages were required – but she knew they'd be much smaller for the younger and more slightly built Clarice. She had no clue whether or not hemlock and cannabis interacted or how they might do so. Was there any way to get it back? Unbelievably reckless. Guilt! She felt guilty, ashamed, immoral. In fact, in a flood, she felt a hundred things she'd never felt before – and it took all her strength to push them away. Her mind asserted control, yet one word remained. Unconscionable. And this was poorly interpreted, her thoughts turning away from what she'd done and looked toward how she'd done it. Bullets were better. Blood. Blood was a guarantee. Blood guaranteed identity and death. She should have done as she'd done in the past and gone with blood.

Blood. Again she was taken by her focus on blood. And again, she failed to understand it.

"Oh... God..." Josie moaned, sitting now with her hands over her face.

"Josie...?" Gabe could see that she hadn't realized he'd been talking to her, maybe didn't fully apprehend that he was even there.

"Blood..."

"Josie!" She slowly turned her head toward him, puzzlement and pain in her face.

"Josie. Wh't happened? Are ya okay? Ah don' see no blood nowhere. But ya might a taken quite a lick when ya fell. Ken ya git up?"

He helped her to her feet and to the rocker nearest the kitchen. She just sat and stared, her mind frantically trying to work through what she had done and whether it was possible to fix it.

"Ah'm gonna fix ya some coffee an' sit with ya awhile till yer a tad bit more normal like."

She sat for a moment, hoping she could get her head straight, hoping Clarice would be okay. She should have realized that even though Clarice wasn't interested in sex, it didn't mean she had no interest in her mother's other activities, and may even have found them useful to cope with her situation.

"Stupid!"

"Josie. Josie. Look at me. Are ya okay? 'Coz ya ain't makin' no sense."

It took effort to focus, to force herself into this moment, this time and space.

"Yes."

"Yes, whut?!"

"Yes. I'm okay."

"Whut happened?"

"I don't know. I fell and knocked myself out... Or... I fainted and fell... Or... I'm not sure..."

"Well ya damn well better git sure er it's gonna happen again, ya hear?!"

"I, uh, maybe I haven't had anything to eat today... Or maybe it's the flu..."

"Well, ya either et er ya ain't et! Which is it?!"

"Um. I ain't et. I mean I haven't eaten."

"Well. La-de-dah. Ah'll git ya sumpin."

Gabe found the staples of Josie's snack diet, peanut butter and crackers, fixed a couple for her, and waited to see her get them down. She still didn't seem quite normal, but there was some improvement. He thought she was a little dazed. Gabe would have made a terribly grouchy nurse, but he was an excellent friend. He sat with her till near dark. She said nothing.

"Ah think ya oughta git ta bed. Mebbe tomorra'll be better. Ah'll check in on ya in the mornin'."

The whole episode was unsettling for Gabe. He'd never seen Josie in such a state and he had seen her with the flu. He couldn't fathom what might be wrong with her. Though he suspected she was too old for such things, he finally laid it to "female trouble", about which he knew nothing. He simply had no other guesses.

Josie was relieved when he left. She hoped it would help her think better. But it didn't. Everything was a question. The questions didn't lead anywhere. Emotions cluttered her thinking until they suffocated it entirely. The structure of her mind had always been much like files, flowcharts, maps, and boxes. Now it was beset with clouds of deepest color – fluid, chaotic, blinding. She wanted to flee but could see no route of escape. Never before had she felt such confusion and horror.

She lacked even the clarity and comfort of kush, having given all of it to Reba. Perhaps it was the recognition of this irony that allowed her mind to begin to clear.

She knew Reba wouldn't return the tainted pot to her. She knew she couldn't steal it back. Clarice was always there so she couldn't sneak in. And even if she could, she'd have no idea where in that packrat mess it might be.

She could turn herself in, confess what she'd done, put it in the hands of law enforcement. But she knew Reba would lie about having received such a thing and the cops would have no better luck at finding it than she would. It might not even be in the house. Besides, this was Mac County. No one would bother to try. One less whoring hillbilly and her dirty offspring wouldn't cause so much as a wrinkled brow, let alone paperwork or an investigation.

Besides, there were still a couple things Josie had left to do.

Two Corpses

By THE TIME GABE LEFT Josie's house, it was over –
too late for anyone to turn the clock back.

Clarice had watched television all day trying not
to think about how hungry she was. Reba never
thought about whether Clarice ate or whether there
was anything for her to eat. If Reba herself was hungry,
she'd buy food, and if she ate at home, she'd grudgingly
share with Clarice. If not, not. This put Clarice in the
odd position of never wanting to see her mother and
wanting to see her, preferably when she was hungry, at
least once a day. The best days for Clarice then were
when her mother smoked pot at home, or at least
returned home shortly after having done so
somewhere else.

Clarice had seen her mother in the late
afternoon carrying a paper bag. It had to be drugs, as
small as it was, as carefully as Reba was tending to it,
as delighted as Reba seemed to be to have it. Saying
nothing to Clarice, Reba regarding her as little more
than the piles of rubbish that rimmed the inner
perimeter of the house, Reba hurriedly found an old
blanket, wrapped it around her shoulders, took her bag,
and left – walking. She couldn't be planning to go far.

Clarice was hopeful that Reba would return home before too long armed to combat the munchies.

That had been hours ago. It was now on the darker side of twilight and her mother had not returned.

Clarice did what she usually did – she rummaged around for her tiny hidden stashes of left over munchie food, found a few chips and a candy bar, ate them, and went to bed. If her mother didn't turn up by the time her stash was gone, she'd go see what Jewel was cooking. She'd done that before. She was a survivor.

On her way home from Josie's, Reba saw Luther's son, Leroy, laid back against his front porch step pitching small rocks at the telephone pole beside the drive. Shirt front open and pants hung low, Reba could see the firm youthfulness of his chest and abdomen. Reba never paid much attention to hair and faces, so Leroy's pimples and greasy hair went unnoticed. She thought to herself that the contents of her bag might slow him down enough to make him a worthwhile lay.

It was to him that she returned with her blanket and her bag. He hadn't moved.

"Yer dad aroun'?"

"Nope." And Leroy scored a hit, ricocheting a rock from the pole back toward the roof of his porch. He smiled.

"Ah's hopin' we might have some fun together."

"Well, he ain't here." Leroy hit again, his long arms having achieved a knack for pelting poles after a whole day of doing nothing else.

"Ah got sumpin' real good in this here bag. Sumpin' what makes fun even funner."

"He ain't here. Don' know when he'll be here neither."

Reba realized this kid would need more tutoring than the average male, as oblivious as he appeared to be to the opportunity at hand. She tried again.

"Well, if yer ole man ain't here, would you be in'erested in fun?"

"Whut kinda fun?"

"Jesus Christ!!! Yer 'bout the dumbest fuck ah ever seen!!!"

Leroy sat up straight as the idea Reba was proposing finally clicked into place. Still, he was hesitant.

"Ah'd sure hate ta make 'im mad. He ken be mean when he's mad."

"So why does he hafta know? Don' appear ta me he's keepin' close tabs on ya."

This was true. Luther had about as much interest in Leroy as Reba had in Clarice, but he was meaner when he was drunk.

Reba smiled as sweetly and charmingly as her features would allow.

"Won't take long. Y'll be home afore 'im. Besides, ah got sumpin special ta make fun funner."

Leroy was no stranger to weed. He'd cabbage onto some of his dad's from time to time if he thought he could get away with it. He was only a beginner at sex though. Reba kind of scared him.

"C'mon."

Leroy slowly stood, straightened himself, pitched one last pebble at the pole, missed, and followed Reba out of his yard.

They walked back to Reba's place, not bothering to make chitchat, bypassed her house, and went toward the woods at the back of her place. In an opening among the oak trees just large enough to admit a little sunlight, she spread her blanket, and brought out her bowl and weed. She opened the bag, took a sniff – a little puzzling but still pleasant – and packed her bowl with enough to share. It was a little sticky, but she got that sometimes and it didn't alarm her. She lit it, took a big deep drag, and passed it to Leroy. He had the lung capacity of youth and drew in for several slow seconds. Feeling themselves dizzy almost immediately, they took it as a good sign, and both had another hit.

Leroy had a seizure. Reba gasped for air. And so it rolled, a series of miserable side effects for a couple hours, till they were both still, breathless, and quite dead.

Even long after full dark, Clarice didn't bother looking for her mother, assuming she was bedded down somewhere and the eating had taken place without her. In fact, no one looked for either Reba or Leroy for several days, until Luther began to wonder what had become of his son. He drove down the road, stopping at each neighbor along the way to ask if they'd seen him. Only the ever vigilant and astonishingly nosy Cecil could report that he'd seen the two of them a few days back walking together. Luther went immediately from there to Reba's, only to find Clarice had no idea where her mother was. Luther, having been to the little clearing in the woods, went to check it out.

What he saw brought no tears. He never cared much for either of them. Leaves and dirt had begun to blow over them, and they were covered with crawling bugs. Even so, and yet still and stiff as they now were, it was obvious from their positions and frozen expressions that they had not gone peacefully. It was a puzzle. All the same, he knew it would be better to look around for himself before he involved the law – if he decided that involving the law might actually help – which it ordinarily did not. He carefully and calmly kicked around in the leaves and grass, looked under the blanket, widened his search a few feet to account for scatter due to wind or woodland critters.

After about half an hour, a tiny glimmer of light flickered dimly from the stem of Reba's brass pipe. The bowl still contained a bit of weed, meaning they died before they finished smoking. Out of habit, Luther absentmindedly took a whiff and found it a bit out of the ordinary. His curiosity piqued, and his mind working furiously, he focused on trying to find more. Nothing. He wasn't a squeamish man, but he was somewhat repulsed at moving dirty buggy dead bodies. But there was nothing else that could be done. He got onto his knees, and with some effort rolled Reba over onto her stomach to discover the bag of remaining weed squashed under her fat ass. He opened it, peered inside, and took another whiff. It wasn't bad, but it wasn't quite right either. A pesticide maybe? That could do it. It happened sometimes.

And then he realized he didn't really care. He rolled Reba back to her original position, dropped the pipe and the bag, and decided to call the law. Let them deal with the cleanup.

He walked back to the house and told Clarice simply, "Yer ma is dead. Died doin' drugs an' fuckin' Leroy. Sorry 'bout that. Ah'll go home an' call the law. Ya should git packed whutever ya wanna take with ya ta foster care."

Clarice stared at Luther for a moment, then asked, "Ya got anythin' on ya ah could eat?"

Luther rummaged around in his truck for a minute and came up with a half-eaten tube of crackers. He tossed them to Clarice, turned, and left.

And Mac County was on the hook for paying for two more burials and caring for one more kid. No other expenditure of time, money, or effort seemed warranted.

KILLING THE WRONG THINGS

JOSIE FOCUSED ON HER WEAVING, all wandering reds and blues, new patterns emerging because old patterns and sequences couldn't be followed or remembered. She saw her work only through a haze of worry that sharpened the colors and blurred the lines. Day and night she worked the treadles and threw her shuttles, stopping to drink coffee, eat peanut butter and crackers, and doze in her rocker when she became so weary she feared falling from her weaving bench. She didn't know how many days had passed.

She had considered riding Selah past Reba's place but knew it wouldn't provide information given that the windows were always covered. She would see nothing and it would tell her nothing. She thought about going right up and knocking on the door, but couldn't think what might come after that. Would it be answered? By whom? What would she say? If it wasn't answered, what should be done next? What if someone saw her? What should she do? Oh, God, what had she done?! And quite literally, she had an answer for none of those questions.

When Gabe came through the door, it was her first clue that it was morning of another day. Without looking at her, he poured himself a cup of coffee, took a sip, emptied it into the sink with the rest of the pot, and brewed a fresh batch. Then he looked at Josie.

She'd been even quieter and more distracted than usual the past few days, but now she looked positively ill.

"Whut's a matter with ya? Ya look like death warmed over. Didja sleep last night?"

"I've been working on my weaving. Deadlines. Promises. Gotta get these done."

"Well, damned if ah can see what'd be so all fired urgent 'bout a rug!"

"Contracts. Commissions. It's a business, Gabe."

"Well, all ah gotta say is there's a lot more important stuff than rugs goin' on in the world."

Gabe waited for his coffee and Josie continued to weave.

"The weather sure has turned off fine the past few days. Jack's already plowed his garden. So's the Bartkins. Ah'm purty sure they's plannin' on gettin' their taters in here in the next few days."

Josie had no comment for this.

"Are ya gonna grow any veg'ables this year? Seems like ya oughta plant stuff ya ken eat! Yer always fussin' aroun' with whut looks ta me ta be weeds. Do ya know yer growin' stuff that other folks're tryin' ta kill? Ya knowed that, right? Wouldn't su'prise me if ya wasn't killin' stuff other folks was tryin to grow!"

Gabe's efforts at humor never garnered much of a reaction, and, in truth served only his own amusement, but Josie seemed to be pondering his joke somehow, so he went on.

"That there's the problem with ya, Josie. Yer killin' all the wrong things!"

Josie sat stark still and stared straight ahead.

Gabe worried that he'd hurt her feelings somehow. Maybe her dye herbs meant more to her than he realized.

"Ah'm sorry, Josie. Ah knowed ya need 'em fer dyein'. Ah was jes funnin' ya."

Josie said nothing. Gabe sat for a minute then thought it might be best to just change the subject.

"Have ya heard the latest news? This here road is shor' seein' its share a dead folks lately! It's a dad-burn epidemic, if ya ask me. One after t'other, they's goin'. This time they was two of 'em. They's jes like all the rest of 'em though. I reckon they ain't much of a loss. Still, ya hate ta see it when one of 'em is so gol-durn young."

Josie steadied herself against the breast beam of her loom

Gabe paused, not sure if Josie was ill, or if she was listening, or if her feelings were still hurt.

"Ah said ah's sorry, Josie. Ah don' know whut else ah ken say. It was jes a joke."

Josie gathered herself.

"Go on with your gossip. Who..."

"Ya know tha' whore up the road? Reba? Well, it was her."

Josie screamed, "Clarice?!! Is Clarice...???!!!"

"Good lord, Josie! Ah di'n't think ya knowed 'em all that well. Ya wasn't friends, was ya?! Josie, Reba tweren't much of a human bein'. Caused a lot a trouble 'mongst married folks in these parts. Ah thought ya knowed all that. They's enough men stoppin' by here, flappin' their gums, tellin' tales."

"CLARICE???!!!!!"

"Jes what ya'd expect, Josie! They tooken her to foster care! Good lord, woman! Whaddya think they'd do? Kill her 'cause her mom took a flop in the woods with Luther's boy, Leroy? What's a matter with ya?"

"Leroy...?"

"Deader 'n a hammer right alongside Reba. It's Luther whut found 'em. He don' seem none the worser fer it. And Leroy showed ever' sign a growin' up ta be jes like his dad. They's worse 'uns fer shor', but that whole lot's purty much no 'ccounts. All a 'em walkin' that line twixt legal and illegal, fallin' off on the wrong side more often 'an not."

Josie and Gabe wandered in their own thoughts for a few moments, Gabe thinking the topic closed.

"Do they know…?"

"Who know whut?"

"How they died? What killed them?"

"Ah reckon not. Prob'ly drugs. Nobody cares, Josie. It ain't worth figgerin' out. Ya been here long 'nough ta know that."

Gabe paused, searching his mind for more information, given that Josie seemed so unusually interested.

"That there Cecil said he seen it comin'. He said he seen 'em tagether an' they looked like they's up ta no good. 'Course, Cecil thinks ever'one's up ta no good. He prob'ly even thinks that 'bout you!"

Gabe thought this might make Josie smile, but it didn't, so he went on.

"That dumb ole Cecil thinks they o-d'ed on pot cuz tha's whut he foun'. He's that stupid. Ever'one else figgers it was sumpin else though cuz pot ain't never killed no one. They di'n't check fer nuthin'. Ah don' know, but mebbe they was too long dead. More'n likely, they jes figgered it wasn't worth it. Anyways, Cecil says that even corpses that's gone stiff and bug eaten is still way better'n the other ones he's cleaned up here lately."

Gabe found himself needing a breath of fresh air, and Josie appeared to be back to her usual way of barely listening, so he left.

All of sudden Josie was more exhausted than she'd ever been in her life. She left her weaving bench to take the rocker next to Gabe's and within minutes she was sound asleep. When Gabe returned in late afternoon, she was still sleeping, but her color was better and he decided there was nothing to worry about after all.

When she awoke, Josie was clear in her mind about one thing: blood was a marker that counted. It was sure. It was the person who bled that was dead. No one could argue with that.

And in the oddest of ways, Josie was acutely aware of her feelings and surprised to find they were in accord with her thoughts. For the first time in many, many years, she pushed neither away from her.

She expected her twilight ride this evening would be better than it had been for several days.

LUTHER REPORTS

LUTHER CALLED THE COPS, waited for them to arrive, watched them kick around the same area in the same way he had done – locating the same items he had located, helped them load the bodies out, and didn't attempt to feign grief. He signed some sort of papers. He assumed it regarded identification of the deceased, but he couldn't read well enough to be certain about it. To Luther's mind, this was sad – sure enough – but it wasn't tragic; and he had no problem admitting to himself that he'd likely miss Reba more than he'd miss Leroy – Reba being more of a pleasant habit and Leroy being more of a benign nuisance.

It seemed like it took CB and Cecil forever to call the coroner and get the bodies loaded out, but he guessed they were trying to show respect they didn't feel or some sort of give-a-damn they didn't have, and he waited for the scene to play out. Luther decided to think of this waste of time as standing some sort of vigil for the deceased – which was appropriate given that there would be no service or memorial or anything like that. Even though Leroy was his son, he was of age and he was the county's responsibility. The county didn't do ceremony. They did cremation and unmarked graves.

Finally they completed whatever official business they thought they were doing, or pretending to do, and left. Luther drove directly to Jack Delevan. There were things Jack needed to know.

Luther was a little afraid of Jack, and not without reason. Luther had crossed him once and he still bore the scars under his beard and he had fewer teeth than he would have had otherwise. Even so, he had gotten off easy and he and Jack both knew it. Ever after, Luther had done everything within his power to either stay on Jack's good side or stay out of his way altogether.

He slowly rolled into Jack's driveway, crunching flint and spreading a low cloud of dirty yellow clay dust. Stopping well back from where he could see Jack working, he sat at the wheel of his pickup for a couple minutes trying to decide what he had to say and whether it mattered how he said it.

Jack was bent over a half dead calf trying to coax it to live with his rough ministrations while cursing its bovine mama and his own human wife under his breath. Why did Jewel insist on dragging home every almost corpse of every species?! Who made her fixer-of-the-universe's problems?! And what gave her the right to rope him in on her missionary tours over Mac County?! For god's sake why didn't she just mind her own fucking business?! It wasn't like they didn't have problems of their own! So, it was an angry and exasperated face he turned toward Luther when he realized he was there.

The mood was such that he almost came to blows with Luther before either of them knew why.

"What the hell ya slinkin' 'roun' ma place fer, Luther?! Ain't ya got stuff ya oughta be doin'? Ain't there no one left in the whole fuckin' county ya can find ta steal off of?!"

Luther didn't answer the question because it didn't really seem to be one. Instead he just started saying what he'd come to say. His gifts, if such they were, ran along the lines of straight-up theft. He wasn't a word guy and he knew it.

"Leroy's dead."

"Goddamn it... I'm sorry, Luther." Jack words were low, slow, and genuine in their sentiment.

"Reba, too."

"Jesus... ...wha...." Now Jack was staggered by the news. He didn't think too much of either one of the deceased and he loathed Luther. Still, this was not only sad – it was alarming.

"Pot."

"What?!"

"Pot kilt 'em. Dirty weed. Dirty with sumthin' I ain't never seen – an' ah seen a lot. Ah could smell it."

"Weed?!"

Luther nodded his head.

"Weed?" Jack asked again, calmer now.

"Yep. Ah foun' it 'fore ah called the cops – an' ah don' know if'n it's right er not, but ah lef' it there."

Jack was trying to collect his thoughts and he stood staring at Luther, looking for whatever signs there might be, considering reasonable possibilities.

"Why? Why do ya think it was the pot?"

"Ah smelt it. An it was the on'y thing aroun'. Had ta be drugs of some kin'. Reba ner Leroy neither one ain't never been sick a day in their lives. An' they was both feelin' up enough fer a tumble. An' they wasn't able ta finish it. An' ya know they wouldn't a wasted it."

Luther was a thief – and he'd steal anything – but for all that, he wasn't a stupid man, and Jack couldn't fault his thinking, especially the last bit. Only death from the weed would leave weed in the bowl.

"What'd it smell like?"

"Sweet? Ah don' know. Green sorta like."

"Did it look funny? Was it dusty?"

"Nope. A little sticky, mebbe?"

Both men pondered the questions: Who tainted it? And with what? And worst, what if there was more?

Luther wanted to leave. If Jack got mad, he didn't want to be around.

"Ah jes thought ya oughta know. An' ya know ah wouldn'ta tole ya iff'n ah had anythin' ta do with it."

Jack looked at Luther again, took in what he said, and acknowledged that it was likely true. He nodded.

"Ah don' wanna end up dead in the woods or floatin' face down in some mine shaft over in Kansas."

Jack nodded again.

He couldn't let Luther off easy and he couldn't afford to let Luther feel comfortable about him. Only Luther could drop the hammer on Jack and his business, because other than his associates, Luther was the only one who knew Jack's business. That's what had gotten Luther his beating. Nosing around Jack's place late one night, looking for something to steal – and the virtue of a stolen article was held entirely by its ease of resale and difficulty of tracing – he happened upon a stash of grass the magnitude of which he could barely comprehend. He planned to take only a relatively small amount, but enough to keep him in money for a month. Or he would have – if Jack hadn't caught him in the act. If it had been one of Jack's associates who'd caught him, Luther would be dead – and Luther knew it.

In a way, that god-awful beating was a kindness. Jack dealt with his problems himself, but for him it was different – though he didn't share this with Luther – and after his beating, Luther didn't suspect it. While it was quite true that Jack was capable of killing, he was not capable of just walking off and forgetting it. And that is a monumental difference.

Without further conversation, Luther turned and left, slowly backing out of Jack's driveway the way he'd come in. He figured he'd done the best he could. At least he was pretty certain Jack wouldn't kill him. He had no idea what his superiors might do – or even who they were.

After he left, Jack resumed tube-feeding the calf and it seemed to be perking up. Maybe there was hope.

At the end of the day, after evening chores and supper, he visited the barn, the silo, and various outbuildings, rummaging in places no one knew about. He'd become much more adept at hiding things since his first problems with Luther. He pulled out samples, sniffed, rubbed them between his palms, sniffed again, lit small amounts, sniffed again. Nothing. This stuff was what it had always been. It might not be top shelf, but it was clean of poison.

Maybe they'd never know what happened to Reba and Leroy. Or why. The bad weed sure as hell hadn't come from any local sources. And it seemed unlikely to Jack that it was just an accident. But he didn't think it would affect his business or anyone in it. And that was good enough. Jack pondered these realities and, in the gentle glow of his nighttime buzz, made his peace with it.

But the peace didn't last. There remained a smoldering worry.

GABE SUSPECTS

HE TOLD GABE he'd already done everything he knew
how to do – he'd cussed it and kicked it – and that he'd
used every tool he had – various sized hammers – and
the damn thing still wouldn't run. Would Gabe mind
dropping by and having a look at his tractor? Gabe
agreed and hoped that Jack had not been "working" on
his tractor too long before he'd made the call.

Jack and Gabe had been neighbors for decades,
though Jack was the younger man by about fifteen or
twenty years. Gabe saw Jack, and his wife Jewel, as
folks who subsisted on the razor's edge between
middle class stable and starving to death. They might
have been more steady, more secure, if Jewel hadn't
always been reaching so high. Or so it seemed to Gabe.
Standing on tiptoe is not a solid position. She dreamed
up scheme after scheme, all of which were entirely legal
(in as far as her understanding of such things allowed),
highly creative, and absolutely unworkable. She paid
down hard-earned money to set them in motion, and
never seemed to notice the money was simply lost time

155

and time again. But she was a good woman, always helping out anyone in need, and taking in anyone with a sob story. Still, Gabe thought Jack the better of the two. Even though it was Jewel who helped, it was Jack who paid the bills for it. Evidently he loved that woman. No matter how much it cost. But in his mind Gabe had to concede that Jack had his defects, too, including a temper toward things, and people, that didn't work.

Mercifully, Jack's frustration had resulted only in cosmetic damage to the already faded old tractor, and Gabe was able to coax it to life again after about an hour and a half of trouble-shooting and tinkering. Relieved, Jack offered Gabe a beer and a bowl, and Gabe accepted the brew but declined the smoke. Leaning against the tractor, in the sweet smelling shade of a persimmon grove, they exchanged neighborhood gossip, in the casual broad strokes men are prone to use.

"Diddja hear 'bout Reba an' Leroy?" Gabe asked.

"Yep. Not much of a loss, the way ah seen it."

"Ah guess not. Unusu'l though, wouldn'tja say?"

The cloudy uneasiness Gabe had been carrying around in his head seemed to be looking for a way out. He finished his beer and squeezed the can into a flat of metal. Looking at it, instead of Jack, he began again, hoping to clear his mind.

"Lot a dead folks 'roun' here lately."

"Don't seem mor'n usual ta me."

"Well, ther's Duke, an' 'en Newt."

"Yeah. But those been a while back."

"An' 'en Tiger."

"That was a mess."

"Huck."

"So wha's yer point?"

"An' now Leroy an' Reba. Jes' seem like a lot."

"Ah guess i's a lot. But we both know not a single one a those sons-a-bitches was worth a shit."

Jack filled his bowl again, threw Gabe another beer, and popped the top on a second one for himself. Gabe felt that he'd just as well go on. He couldn't stand what had been in his head for so long and he was determined to get it out and examine it in the light of day.

"Don' 'at seem mighty coincidental? All 'ese dead folks was *bad* dead folks? Don' it seem like sometimes the dead folks oughta be *good* dead folks?"

"What the fuck are ya talkin' 'bout?! Whaddaya mean, 'there oughta be good dead folks'?!"

"Well, ah was jes' sayin' tha' accidents oughta come along kinda reg'lar like – tha' if'n i's on'y bad folks doin' the dying, that... Well... Ah don' know..." and there was no place to go but to the end of the thought, "It almos' look like they's bein' hepped along in some way... by somebody..."

"Jesus, Gabe! It looks ta me like the wrath of God is visitin' Mac County an' i's high time, too!"

Gabe sighed. "Mebbe."

"'sides, they was Lily an' 'at slow Bennett kid. Ya cain't say they's bad, but they's shor' 'nuff dead."

"Yeah. Ah guess, so."

Jack could see that Gabe had more to say but was having second thoughts about saying it.

"Okay. Out with it. Whut other crazy ideas ya got floatin' aroun' in 'at head a yers?"

Gabe really didn't want to go on, but he craved relief from the poorly formed suspicions he had.

"Notice anythin' in common with these dead folks other than badness?"

"No."

"Ya know ole Monroe an' Goldie's daughter, Josie?"

"Yeah. Seems nice 'nuff. Ah stop by once in awhile when ah have the time an have a cup a coffee with her an' see how she's doin'. We've had some dealin's. She seems nice enough."

"Well, ah stop by an' visit her 'most every day. Sometimes twicet a day."

"Gabe! I di'n't know ya had it in ya!"

"It ain't like 'at!"

"Okay! Okay. Whatever ya say. Ah di'n't mean ta git ya riled up. Go on with whut ya's saying."

"Well, most a the dead folks live on land whut borders Josie's."

"So? She's got a big piece a land. It borders a lot a folk's places. It borders mine. Most a the other big places was chopped up a long time ago. Jes' happens hers wasn't. Ah don' see whut tha' has ta do with anythin'."

Gabe dropped his empty can and stomped it. He felt stupid. Why couldn't he just leave it there? Gabe wasn't even sure he had any suspicions. He had only gaps, blank spaces, questions, and he could articulate none of these. But it had begun to seem that every time that Josie was faint or pukey or off-normal in any way, someone had just died. Only recently had he begun to realize that he knew almost nothing about Josie. It was as if she were some kind of bird that he'd seen a thousand times, but knew nothing of its migration patterns, mating rituals, nesting habits. It was an all too seldom acknowledged, all too common occurrence, a mental condition wherein profound familiarity masks profound ignorance.

"Jack, there's sumpin' strange 'bout it."

"Like what?" Jack peered through the blue smoke and saw the answer on Gabe's face. "Ya don' think she had anythin' ta do with any of 'em, do ya? Do ya?!"

Gabe could say no more.

Jack lowered his voice. He was about to say more than he wanted to, but these two men, though not close, trusted one another.

"Gabe, ah knowed who kilt Duke an' Newt both. Ah ain't so's ah ken talk 'bout it. But ah know. An' ah know tweren't Josie. As fer as Tiger goes, ah don' know anyone thinks a bush hog is a reliable murder weapon. Same fer dogs. Ah don' see how's them las' two is anyways sim'lar anyhow. They wasn' a soul in this worl' give two shits 'bout Tiger an' they musta been a hun'erd men achin' bad to kill Huck. Besides, ah don' think this woman even knowed 'em."

Gabe's mood seemed to lighten, so Jack went on. Then his own questions about Reba and Leroy drifted into mind. He pushed them back.

"Ah'll allow that Leroy an' Reba is a puzzle. Mebbe ya ken pin 'em on 'er, but ah don' see how."

At first Jack thought the entire conversation was ridiculous, but Gabe seemed so upset, and tangled up in his thinking somehow. Jack had never seen him like this. He didn't know what to think.

"Gabe, ya sure ya ain't messing aroun' with this woman? Because ya shore seem that kin' a messed up in yer head."

"Ah swear ta god ah ain't touched her!"

And Jack believed him. Still, she was in his head somehow.

Jack didn't want to think about it. No matter how hard he tried to mind his own business, no matter how little interest he had in the goings on of other folks, he seemed to be in the smack middle of too many things. And, of course, it was his aversion to the problem that caused the problem. He had grown up in this neighborhood. So had Jewel. They were raising Alice here amongst her friends and schoolmates, most of whom got off the bus with her in hopes of sharing Jewel's fresh baked cookies and cupcakes. Nearly all of them called Jack "Pa" because Alice did and because Jack allowed it. These facts alone meant he was too deeply intertwined in the tangle of life hereabouts that he would never be free to simply mind his own business and go his own way. He knew everyone for several miles around given the marryings and birthings of siblings, nieces, nephews, and in-laws. Plus, with Jewel's inclination to take in wayward souls, and her general hospitality to anything that breathed, it wasn't surprising that many folks in the neighborhood considered themselves family members.

Jack wanted to blame Jewel for entanglements, except for the simple truth that it wouldn't be possible for her to do what she did without his support. In fact, she required every kind of support he could provide – physical, emotional, financial. He loved her. He would do anything for her, anything within his power. There was more. He didn't admit it, even to himself. It would be too unmanly, too weak, to admit he cared as much as she did about their strays, the only difference being that she had the freedom to show it. In his mind, he did not.

Nevertheless, care he did. He wished Gabe had never confided in him. It prayed on his mind. It hadn't seemed like anything unusual until Gabe pointed it out. People died. They died too soon and too late, peacefully and violently. That was the way of it. Jack had lived here all his life, known all his neighbors for most of their lives, known the heartbreak and the hilarity. Some things were sad and some things were stupid and most things weren't anything at all. Just living. And dying was part of that.

He also understood murder better than most folks did. So for reasons of his own, reasons far more powerful than Gabe's, he began to wonder about Josie, too.

Or someone.

CECIL

CECIL SPENT MOST OF HIS TIME WORKING – he'd
rather be anywhere than home – and most of the time
he spent working he was trying to fend off boredom.
It is a sad truth in the world that people who are
chronically bored, who have virtually nothing going on
in their own lives, fill the void by becoming intensely
interested in the goings on in the lives of others. In
other words, instead of actually finding something to
do, they spend their days listening to gossip,
propagating gossip, and filling their quiet times musing
over improbable scenarios wherein other folks are the
players. All of this was true of Cecil. Plus, he had a
badge.

Perhaps, like many others with the same habits,
he should be forgiven for it – and his mother blamed
instead. Mildred Gravis was about the most unlikeable
person it's possible to meet. She was the very definition
of imperious, feeling it her right to command those
beneath her and thinking everyone she met was rightly
placed upon that lower level. Her own elevated
position she attributed to the grace of God – in that
He recognized her righteousness and blessed her with
exceptional insight and ability.

Mildred, being the saintly mother she was,
forever busied herself helping her son to be a better
person, the person he was destined to be, the mirror of
her own attributes. To this end she nagged – she would

have said "encouraged" – Cecil to be immaculate in his habits, impeccable in his manners, and unfailing in radiating his birthright of superiority. At home, he was continually monitored in every detail of his actions.

"Cecil, a gentleman takes smaller bites and chews slower so there is no noise. Try again with your next bite. There. That's better."

"Cecil, a gentleman keeps his socks pulled up so his shins don't show when he sits. If you can't manage it with those socks, go put on another pair."

"Cecil, how long has it been since you tidied your hair today? You're an officer of the law. There are certain expectations. Don't smooth it with your hand. Use a comb. Don't dress your hair in public. Go to the bathroom. Besides there's a mirror in there."

"Cecil, when is the last time you properly shined your shoes? I know you go places where it's dusty, but that's no excuse."

"Cecil, I can hear you turn the pages when you read and it's very distracting. I'm trying to read myself. Could you be a little more thoughtful?"

And so on. And on. When he was at home, there literally wasn't one single thing Cecil could do right. From his childhood he had been subjected to her efforts toward his improvement. His father had been encouraged and improved to an early grave. This was the environment in which Cecil had been raised. He did his best to please the woman because it was so easy for her to progress from helpful comments to full blown rages to guilt-inducing hysterical weeping. Most of the neighborhood had heard the rages and the closest neighbors had heard the weeping. For their part, the neighborhood viewed Mildred as insane and Cecil as to be pitied – despite the fact that his mother kept his clothes and her house and their yard in faultless condition.

Still, being pitied and being liked are two very different things. While folks on the road understood and sympathized with Cecil's desire to avoid his home, that didn't mean they wanted him hanging around theirs. Similarly, they felt that having no business of his own didn't entitle him to be snooping around in theirs. In sum, they didn't hate him, didn't like him, and didn't know what to do about his nosiness. Their feelings were much akin to the teeth-gritting attitude folks have toward unrelenting rodent problems in their houses. The fact that he was a sheriff's deputy didn't help.

Cecil had the time to be intrigued in everyone's business, but as CB had hoped, he wasn't terribly bright. As such, CB mostly ignored whatever suspicions and findings Cecil brought to his attention. Over time Cecil stopped consulting CB, hoping that someday he would astonish him by presenting important results of his investigative efforts.

Surprisingly, despite their differences in age, personality, and abilities, Cecil's suspicions had quite a lot in common with Gabe's, though he didn't have any particular suspect in mind.

Given his churchly upbringing and his mama's admonitions, he had never gotten the knack of seeing things in shades of gray. For him, as for many others in that part of the world, things were seen in black and white. There was right and wrong. There was good and evil. There were blessings and punishments. There was divine intervention writ in bold letters. There were no coincidences, no accidents, no randomness, no purposelessness, no mysteries. There was God Almighty and the Devil Himself doing battle all over the world, including right here in Mac County. Cecil was both absolutely certain of these things and hopelessly terrified of them – as is usually the case in such clearly delineated belief systems.

He didn't know much about Newt's and Duke's deaths other than rumor. It was before his time with the sheriff's department and the sheriff's department had retained no investigative records, if indeed there had been an investigation. Even so, he was positive that either they were very bad men who quite predictably came to very bad ends, or they were very good men victimized by very bad men who would, in due time, come to predictably very bad ends. There were no other possibilities. Black and white, right and wrong, good and evil were always in direct opposition to one another precisely because God and the Devil were opponents. Reason itself demanded that it could be no other way.

So, when Cecil was called upon to clean up the stringy bloody mess that were the remains of Tiger's corpse, he could see it as nothing other than the work of the Devil and his minions. How had the Devil managed it? Who were his minions? This thinking was strengthened and magnified by the unholy mess he was forced to shovel through looking for pieces of Huck. He knew in his gut – just before his stomach emptied – that this was pure evil. Then, straight from the warnings in the Bible, Cecil was reminded that the Devil could be subtle and it must have been his subtlety that allowed him through his minions to kill Reba and Leroy.

Parked alongside the dead end road, soaking in the sunshine, basking in the superiority he'd inherited from his mama, he was sure he'd been appointed to be the Arm of God in Mac County and he would usher in the clear clean light of a new day.

Fantasies are a great aid for the relief of boredom.

Part 2

<u>Ella</u>

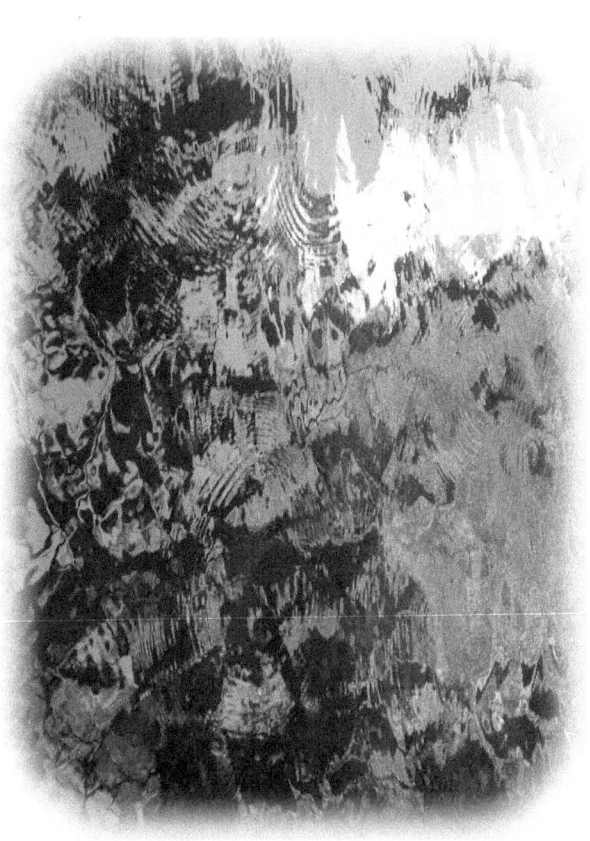

CECIL INVESTIGATES

CECIL BELIEVED HIMSELF SKILLED in the art of subterfuge and a master of subtlety. His neighbors believed him to be a sneak and a liar – and not gifted at either. He would meet them going opposite ways on the road and attempt to get them to stop. Sometimes, he'd flash the lights of his cruiser on and off – by way of friendly reminder that he could write a ticket for those disinclined to have a friendly chat. He had been raised in such a way that spotting tiny things amiss – a missing license plate, malfunctioning turning signals, too noisy mufflers – was as easy and as natural as breathing air.

In the beginning he took great delight in seeing how many tickets per day he could write, until Sonny grabbed a pitchfork from the back of his pickup and ran him through with it. CB declined to file charges given the neighborhood support for Sonny, and Cecil's enthusiasm for ticket-writing waned considerably after he was released from the hospital. Still, most people would stop for Cecil, acknowledge whatever fault in their vehicle or their driving he pointed out, and accept

171

as punishment the thirty minute conversation that was the real reason for being stopped in the first place.

"So, Jewel, I noticed you don't have plates on this old Ford."

"Ah know. It belongs to Mrs. Ideman an' ah'm takin' it ta git tuned up so's ah ken drive her ta visit her husban's grave one las' time. That poor ole woman ain't got nobody an' ah 'spec she knows she ain't long for this world, an' she was cryin' 'bout not gittin' flowers on his grave an' how she jes couln't rest knowin' that. Ah know it ain't no big deal – 'cep' it is ta her. Afterall, it ain't much fer a lady at's lived as long as she has ta ask – and ah aim ta see ta it that her las' days are as happy as ah ken make 'im. An' how's yer mama doin', Cecil? Ah see she's got her marigolds an' geraniums an' begonias planted all purty 'roun' her porch agin this year. She shore is a busy woman – an example ta all of us. Now you tell 'er ah said hi. Ah gotta git goin' now though, er ah won't make it before the garage closes. Plus ah have ta pick up Alice an' take 'er ta git new shoes. Well, ah don' wanna keep ya no longer! Ah know ya got stuff ya gotta do!"

With that Jewel rolled up her car window, started the engine, waved and smiled real big, and left. Cecil was never quite sure what happened when he stopped Jewel, but he knew it happened every time. He seemed to get a lot of information and yet no information at all. In his fantasy, sometimes important nuggets lurked hidden within trivial information. Even so, he sincerely doubted that to be the case with Jewel Delevan. Her talk was always food, flowers, kids, and old folks.

"Hi there Bennett. You probably didn't notice but you pulled right out of your driveway without looking both ways down the road. What if something had been coming?"

172

"Ah reckon ah'd a seen a big ole cloud a dust an' figgered sumthin's in a middle of it."

Cecil couldn't think how to counter this reasoning and decided to drop all pretenses before he became more confused.

"You knew Huxley Evers, right?"

"'Bout ever'one did."

"You worked for him though, right?"

"Fer a couple weeks."

Cecil couldn't think what else to ask, but thought he should keep the conversation going till he could think of something.

"Nice weather, isn't it?"

"Too dry."

"Um."

"Look, Cecil, it's been nice chewin' the fat with ya, but ah got stuff ta do."

"Oh. Okay. Well. See you later then."

Bennett nodded, hoping "later" meant a very long time before he saw Cecil again.

"Hop in Mike, I'll give you a ride. These flint rocks are sure hard on old tires, aren't they? I guess you're walking because you don't have a spare. Do you want me to take you home or to Bob's to see if he has a used tire he can sell you?"

"Jes take me home. Ah'll see whut ah got a layin' aroun' there."

"You live next door to Ruth's place, don't you?"

"Yep."

"How's Ruth handling things now that Tiger's dead."

"A mite more comfor'ble, ah'd guess."

"Did you know Tiger?"

"Ah jes said ah lived next door. Ah din' say we's frien's. Tiger din' have no frien's."

Cecil always worked very hard to keep his tone conversational, not wanting people to realize he was doing actual police work. He needn't have worried. Most folks thought the nasty corpse cleanups had addled his brain – and further, they believed Cecil was decidedly incapable of investigative work – even had it been warranted – which it wasn't.

"Did you know he was going to brush hog, you know, the time he died?"

"How in hell would ah know whut the ole fuck was doin' or 'bout ta do a'fore he got hisse'f kilt?"

And so it went for many months – to the point that on some days Cecil wondered if there weren't a conspiracy of some sort, or worse – and he found this possibility extremely likely – some kind of satanic ritual initiation that involved bloody gruesome killing.

Cecil found himself talking to Gabe more than anyone else. Maybe it was because Gabe had more time on his hands than the average resident, or that he was more reluctant to hurt Cecil's feelings by shutting him down and moving on, or that he was, by his own nature, more inclined toward gossip and speculation. No matter the reason, Cecil found a reliable listener in Gabe, to the extent that Cecil progressed from sharing his questions, to sharing his tidbits, to sharing his speculations – Gabe finding the latter deranged, but a derangement of a type commonly encountered thereabouts.

Eventually Cecil concluded that stopping folks in their vehicles was a useless endeavor. They seemed always to be on their way somewhere! Granted, this should have been obvious from the beginning, but for Cecil, it was something that had to be learned – and it was a blessed relief to everyone on the road when he finally learned it.

So, he began visiting with the non-mobile folks on the road, which meant he spent an inordinate amount of time stopping in to visit with the elderly and the homebound. This is where things became odd for Cecil. For one thing, it tended to improve his standing and likeability among residents; and for another thing, the folks he visited had a greater appetite for chitchat than Cecil did. They had a longer history in, and knowledge of, the neighborhood, and the ability to deliver lengthy stories – pre-embellished with rumor, humor, fantasy, speculation, and opinion. They buried Cecil in information. Cecil knew that parts of what they said were likely true; but to save his life he couldn't tell which parts those might be.

Cecil brought all of this to Gabe, too, or as much of it as he could remember from one visit to the next. Gabe would sometimes nod in agreement, sometimes shake his head in disbelief, sometimes shrug his shoulders, and sometimes laugh till his ribs ached and he couldn't catch his breath – none of which was of any use to Cecil. Cecil finally had to acknowledge that Gabe was never likely to get the point of any of his efforts. There was, however, one happy result, Gabe was beginning to actually like Cecil. A little bit.

Cecil was exasperated. Being nosy is easy. Obtaining useful incriminating information is much more difficult. Due solely to the workings of his own mind, Cecil was convinced that Tiger, Huck, Reba, and Leroy had all been murdered by evil doers and evil doings of some stripe; and that it was his God-given duty to expose these doers and doings to the light of day. He had visions of being the wrath of God in a deputy uniform. Clean and nicely pressed.

He put his head to it. What was left for him to do? His investigation had not progressed. Besides, he'd grown tired of being dust covered by passing cars when he conducted his "traffic stops". He'd grown tired of muddy paw prints from giant mutts at old folks' houses. He'd grown tired of sitting in musty chairs in smelly living rooms listening to toothless stinky old folks. It was time to move beyond these things. It was time to dig in, to embrace the innovative and the daring, to counter the devil's deviousness with enlightened courage. In other words, he decided to start rummaging through people's mailboxes.

He deemed his own plan simple yet brilliant. He knew what time the mailman made his way along RR#5. He knew he couldn't simply drive along behind him rifling through what had just been left. However, he could sit in his cruiser at various vantage points along the road, and learn what times of day residents retrieved their mail. Cecil figured it would take two or three weeks to learn everyone's mail routine. From there it would be relatively straightforward. He'd simply check everyone's mail before they did!

Cecil's training in legal studies from the local community college had not gone so far as to inform him of the illegality of his plan, so he was in no way bothered about it in that regard. Still, he knew it was in his best interests as an investigator to remain undetected. He hadn't forgotten his run-in with Sonny's pitchfork, or the lesson that people get peevish about certain things. It was best that he plan as carefully as possible. He needed to open envelopes and reseal them in such a way that his tampering would go unnoticed.

He planned to dissolve most seals with patience and a damp sponge. He could reseal them with a glue stick. A heavy book to smash them flat again after they'd been resealed would be nice, too. That was it: his "kit" consisted of a small water bottle, a sponge cut into one-inch squares, a couple kindergartener glue sticks, a small spiral bound pad for notes, a mechanical pencil, and a very old dictionary (the latter taken from his mother by explaining to her that he sought to improve his vocabulary during slow times). Cecil kept everything but the dictionary in an old cigar box and fought the idea that it looked like school supplies. He was ready to begin.

It was a jumble at first. It took longer than he thought to open the mail, read it, and return it to its original condition. Then he realized he could simply remove the mail and work on it somewhere more private later in the evening. If he returned the mail to the box the following day, no one would be the wiser.

As for the mail itself, everybody got electric bills, well, almost everybody. He learned they weren't worth the trouble of opening and resealing. Big houses with lots of lights had big electric bills. Smaller houses had correspondingly lower bills, and so on. A lot of folks got bank statements and some folks were absolutely inundated with mail regarding insufficient funds. He was surprised to find that Pancake, an old, old man living in a tarpaper shack, was actually quite wealthy due to some sort of lifetime payment deal associated with a work accident. A fair number of people were on the dole, but there weren't any real surprises there. There were several people who received court notices and had communications with lawyers, but he already knew who these folks were and what the notices were about.

Frankly, it didn't take too long before it all got boring. Nobody knew anyone, nobody did anything, nobody went anyplace. But he had no more ideas and nothing else to do. There weren't any tidbits even worth sharing with Gabe – except for Pancake's wealth – which Cecil pretended to have gleaned from conversation – and which Gabe already knew. Cecil was reluctant to share with Gabe that his investigative methods had expanded to include personal mail. He was reasonably sure it was something a civilian wouldn't understand and might very well resent.

He was about to give up when Josie's mail piqued his curiosity.

He intercepted confirmation of a hotel reservation, a Hilton on the southern edge of Chicago. What business could Josie possibly have in Chicago? He decided to bring it up the next time he talked to Gabe.

"Guess what I found?"

"How would ah know?"

"I found a reservation of Josie's for a hotel in Chicago."

"How'dya 'find' that?!"

"Um. It was in mom's mailbox. Mailman must have made a mistake. I took it and put in Josie's box where it belonged."

"Uh-huh."

Cecil noticed Gabe's disgust, and he was relieved he hadn't told Gabe about what he'd been doing. He plunged ahead.

"What do you think Josie has to do in Chicago?"

"Could be anythin'. She useta live thar. Ah 'spec' she still knows folks thar."

"There's a lot of bad goings-on in Chicago. A big city like that."

It was a common perception in Mac County, especially among the churchly people, that big cities were dens of iniquity, and that a sizeable sum of evil emanated from them. Of course, this perception, when encountered, was very difficult to dislodge given that almost no one had been even so far as Springfield or Kansas City.

"There's a lot a bad goin's-on right chere in Mac County."

"True."

And they both pondered this truth for a moment, though from completely different perspectives. Cecil tried again.

"I wonder if the evil there and the evil here might be connected somehow."

Gabe looked at Cecil as if he'd lost his mind.

"Ah don' know whatcher talkin' 'bout an' ah 'spec' neither do you!"

It was not infrequent that Gabe was the one that cut their conversations short when he thought Cecil had once again crossed the bounds of the rational.

Cecil gave it up. He was the professional here. Gabe was not. Of course Gabe wouldn't be able to see the connection. Cecil was on his own now. Cecil would have to follow Josie to Chicago and continue his investigation there.

It turned out that the nearer Cecil got to the time to be on his own, the less sure he was that he wanted that. His plan was to go to Chicago, to the hotel where Josie had her reservation, and follow her from there. Then he scared himself with his own imagination of that evil city, and decided he'd be better off with some company. But who? He realized that he had no friends, though he didn't express it that way to himself. Both he and his mother thought more in terms of rankings than in relationships, so it was not surprising that they should find themselves more or less alone.

He went to Jack for advice, and was lucky to find him working on his wicker furniture, an activity that tended to render Jack more pleasant and sociable than otherwise.

"I'm planning a trip to Chicago."

"Good fer you. Ah hope ya have fun."

"Well, I've got to take care of some errands there."

Jack kept working on his furniture, paying scant attention to his visitor. It was a necessity. Jack was often subjected to visitors and he couldn't quit working every time someone stopped by. But he was skilled at simultaneously sustaining both the work and a semblance of conversation.

"Ah din't know ya had eny affairs in Chicago."

"It's for the sheriff's department."

"Ah din't know Mac County had eny affairs in Chicago."

"It's to pick up supplies. I probably shouldn't have mentioned it."

And this was a place usual in Cecil's conversations where Cecil got nervous because he was lying – at the precise moment his listeners became aware of the nervous lying as well. This time, like most times, it wasn't considered any more important than Cecil himself was.

"I was hoping to find someone to ride along with me. You know. Kind of keep me company. It's a long trip. I'd buy the meals."

"Soun's nice."

Jack was focused on attaching the legs and back to the seat of a chair with rawhide lashing, and Cecil waited till he had it mostly complete. Jack had forgotten Cecil till he spoke again.

"I was wondering if you might know of someone willing to go."

Jack stood up, arched and stretched his back, and thought about it a few minutes.

"Well, thar's Sonny Richards. He works fer me sometimes an' ah think he's right pleasant company. He might go."

"Sonny Richards??!!! He tried to kill me with a pitchfork!"

"Cecil, if Sonny Richards had a-tried ta kill ya with a pitchfork, ya'd be dead now. Sonny di'n't wanna kill ya. He wanned ya ta leave 'im alone."

"I was in the hospital two weeks!"

"But not in the morgue!"

Jack could see that Cecil was getting excited and he could understand that being skewered with a pitchfork would leave a bad taste in a person's mouth. But he tried to reason with him.

"Look. Sonny's got a temper – 'spec'ally when he's been a-drinkin'. Whaddaya 'spec'? He's one a Quentin's and Lily's young 'uns. But he's done well fer hisse'f. He works purty reg'lar at the feed mill, he ain't a thief – an' he don' pick fights – lessn he's been provoked. He ain't the type ta hold grudges neither. Ba'sides, ah think he's 'bout yer age. Don' provoke him an' don go drinkin with him and ah garntee it'll be jes fine. Plus, he ain't the kin whut's apt to panic an' that there ken come in handy. An' if yer real worried 'bout it, jes don' bring along no pitchfork!"

Jack said the last of it with a grin thinking he'd made a joke that Cecil could appreciate – and then remembered that Cecil wasn't given to joking. Jack went back to his work and began to whistle. Cecil took it as a signal that the conversation was over.

What choices did he have? The problem was how to ask him. He knew it would be best if he didn't stop him along the road with his cruiser.

In the end, Cecil just drove up to his house, the place where his folks used to live and where several of their offspring still did, knocked on the door, asked for Sonny, told him the same story of his plans that he'd told Jack, and asked if Sonny would like to come along. Sonny stared at him a long time, looking for something in this idea that might cause him grief. Espying nothing, he smiled and agreed to go. Mutual boredom is the bedrock upon which many a friendship has been built. And a fair number of mishaps as well. Both Cecil and Sonny began to look forward to the trip.

CECIL GOES TO CHICAGO

CECIL WAS WEARING ORDINARY JEANS and a t-shirt when he picked Sonny up in his mother's Chrysler. (He had told her he was doing undercover work which must be kept very secret. Delighted, she envisioned newspaper headlines and photos of her son with a cuffed modern day Al Capone beside him.) Sonny was somewhat disappointed they weren't going in the police cruiser; and Cecil was somewhat disappointed to see that he and Sonny were in almost identical attire – meaning no one would be able to discern that he was the person of authority, especially since Cecil was a little too frightened of Sonny to attempt to boss him around.

But the trip from Mac County to Chicago is a long one and neither man wanted it to be unpleasant. The tone was easily reset when they both agreed to have breakfast at a truck stop along I-44. As promised, Cecil picked up the tab, and unexpectedly Sonny sprang for a generous tip, earning Cecil's respect as someone who was not entirely socially inept, nor completely destitute.

After they had discussed the weather – past, present, and future – pointed out to one another unusual advertising structures – speculated about how close they'd need to be to St. Louis to see the arch in the distance – there was nothing left to talk about. Finally, foregoing conversational niceties because he was growing very bored, Sonny asked bluntly, "So, why are we going to Chicago?"

Of the two, Cecil was actually the more socially naïve. He had no experience with relationships other than with his mother and Gabe. His understanding of social interactions was that of a child and he believed Sonny was offering to serve as a confidant. Cecil accepted the offer.

As it turned out, and given that his father had murdered his mother, Sonny had no trouble at all believing in the possibility that Tiger, Huck, Reba, and Leroy might have been murdered as well. In fact, he suggested that perhaps Jay, too, had been murdered, and he also remembered stories about Duke and Newt.

Cecil had finally found someone he could talk to! So, Cecil expounded first upon one theory, then another, listened to Sonny's comments, discussed pros and cons of various scenarios, and ranged freely from the possible to the preposterous in their considerations.

In the end, they decided that Josie was the most likely murderer. Their conclusion was based on three damning factors: 1) Josie's land adjoined the land of all the victims – which meant there was something hidden on her land that she was afraid someone close might discover; and 2) She came from Chicago which everyone knew was an evil and violent place – which made her capable of every brutality; and 3) They knew nothing at all about her past – which meant that there must be nothing but evil in it or it wouldn't be secret. The first factor convinced them she had both motive and opportunity, though they acknowledged they were short on specifics for both. As to method, they couldn't be sure, but both were willing to entertain the idea that supernatural forces could very well be at work.

At any rate, they were sure that if they could confront her with a single piece of damning evidence, she would crumple into immediate confession and all would be made clear. The trip had become an adventure and they had become giddily delighted in its pursuit. They were doing surveillance! In addition, Cecil was doing the work of God.

When they arrived in Chicago, they checked into the same hotel where Josie was staying, being careful to park Cecil's mother's car so they had a clear view of Josie's pickup, and could pull out of their space without having to back up. They were too excited to sleep and finally convinced themselves that the best idea would be to wait in the car because they had no idea how early Josie would leave the hotel to go about her nefarious business.

Nefarious is what they expected, but they expected it to look like it always did.

The driver of the rented gray Honda Fit didn't seem to be the same person. The woman who had gotten out of an older model pickup yesterday evening to check into the hotel was Josie. The regular Josie – gray t-shirt, denim overalls, a single silver braid of hair down her back, army green duffle bag slung over one shoulder. Throughout the time they'd known her, they had never seen Josie any other way. It was as if her selection of clothing were her actual skin. It took them several moments to realize this new person was the woman they'd come to follow. Black pencil skirt, black heels of sensible height, blouse of ivory colored silk, maroon suede blazer, hair in a loose French knot at the back of her head, a large black leather handbag – Josie had transformed herself into a stylish affluent professional woman, as unremarkable a person in downtown Chicago as she had been in rural Mac county. It was hard to take it in.

She was already out of her parking spot, out of the lot, and waiting for a light at an intersection before they even got their car started. They didn't know if they'd be able to catch her. Josie was much more adept at handling big city traffic than they were and she had a head start. If Cecil had not spent so much of his idle time playing with the cruiser, experimenting with how it accelerated, how it handled sharp turns, how it could overtake speeders, he wouldn't have had a chance. As it was, even though he had to adapt to the lesser capabilities of his mother's Chrysler, he was sufficiently adept as a driver to catch Josie. It helped that Sonny was able to help keep track of her lane changes and turns.

On Josie's part, she had no idea anyone had an interest in her doings that morning. Somehow in her own mind, Josie wasn't even in Chicago. Josie lived in Mac County on her father's old place, kept a small farm, and lived a simple life. That was there. Josie was there. Doctor Ella J. Dillard was here. In Chicago. In every way, she was a different person here.

TY

WHEN THE "HERE" FOR JOSIE WAS CHICAGO, the time was never now. It was then. A long ago then.

Evidently she had some piece of her father Monroe's wanderlust, because upon graduation from high school Josie applied for, and received, a small scholarship from the University of Missouri at Columbia. She supplemented this with federal financial aid. As restless in her mental wanderings as she was in her physical surroundings, she was, by turns, a chemistry major, a mathematics major, an English major, a psychology major, and a philosophy major. Even so, a shifting focus should not be mistaken for an absent one. Josie loved college. It was a perfect blend of learning and anonymity.

She spent very little time in her dorm room and did not form a close attachment with any of her roommates. On a typical day, she would arise in the early morning and eat in the cafeteria when it was peopled only by a handful of fellow students – mostly a sullen groggy group, but there were a few up early and desperate to meet a deadline looming only hours later. It was here that she developed the habit of watching people, of trying to see into them, speculating as to their motivations and fears, wondering how they'd come to be here in the same room doing the same things. Yet she was never really with them, never part of any group. She recognized the regulars and, gathering tiny hints from what they ate or read, how they dressed or walked or greeted strangers, or not, she felt she knew them. It was not a conscious undertaking, but she became quite proficient at human observation nonetheless. More akin to scientific observation than social interaction, it became, in fact, an addiction, though she never acknowledged it as such – and there would come a day when she so retreated from herself and her own humanity that it would be no longer possible for her to take even this small interest in anyone.

Occasionally, someone with whom she'd had a class would ask to join her and she would smile and acquiesce, make small talk about an instructor or class or campus event, and gather clues about yet another person she had no feelings for. These shared breakfasts were neither better nor worse than her solitary ones.

On the morning Ty joined her, she had completed the paperwork for a change of major the previous day and was still mulling over her decision. His request to join her was a surprise because she had never met him before and had not shared so much as a single class with him. He sat down and began a monologue about how he didn't like eating alone, about how he usually slept in, about a birdwatching field trip he had to join in the next hour, about the demands of being an accounting major, and so on – till his hour wait was nearly spent. It was, by far, the most peculiar personal encounter Josie had ever had. She found him fascinating. As he left, half a slice of toast in hand, Josie wondered if he would be considered good looking by most people and realized she had no way to judge.

Josie would become better at judging. At least when it came to Ty.

There were to be many more breakfasts with him. Josie learned his moods and that, whether good, bad, confused, or happy, they were always high energy. She had rarely seen emotion in her life and to see them thus magnified in a person was exhilarating, though to all outward appearances she was only calmly absorbed in whatever Ty brought to the table in the morning.

It was many months before Ty actually saw Josie sitting across from him. He stopped talking and confronted the fact that there was a face between her listening ears, that the face belonged to a person, that it might be time to get to know the person. After months of talking, it was to be their first real conversation.

"I've been doing all the talking."

Josie smiled, still expecting him to continue.

He stuttered, "I don't even know your full name. Maybe you don't know mine either. I'm Tyson Eugene Dillard. A few people call me Ted because of my initials, but most people call me Ty. I like Ty better."

"Ella Josephine Mansell. People here call me Ella." They made a show of shaking hands.

"Where are you from?"

"The southwest corner of the state. You've never heard of it. McDonald County."

"Is that where your family lives?"

"It's where my parents live. I don't have any brothers or sisters or aunts or uncles or anything like that."

"What's your major?"

"Everything. Currently, it's philosophy. Mostly because it has so many electives that nearly all my other courses count toward graduation."

"How long till you graduate?"

"Probably next year."

It was beginning to feel a bit like an inquisition. Ty tried to bring it back into the realm of normal conversation before he made Ella feel awkward. He thought maybe information reciprocation would make it more like a conversation.

"I was raised in Saint Louis. Dad left Mom when I was little. He sent money like he was supposed to, but that was all. I have a little sister. Well, she's in high school now."

He paused, not knowing where else to go.

"I guess you know all about my major and what I want to do after I graduate. All that stuff."

Ella nodded and smiled at the only understatement Ty had ever made.

"Ella. I like it. I think it's pretty. I think you're pretty." He got up to leave, wondering to himself if his last statement was strictly true.

And wondering about the truth of that statement was the first thing Ella and Ty actually shared.

TY AND ELLA

SEEING TY was always her first order of business when she was in Chicago. Other than college, it was the only place they'd been together. He was present to her here as he would never be in Mac County. In Chicago she could access memories of him that were joyful, passionate, vibrant. In Mac County he was a ghost. He haunted her, taunted her with unanswerable questions. There, he wasn't a person. He was a puzzle.

It had been so few years together and so many years ago, Ella sometimes had trouble grasping that it had been a real time in her life, that it had been really her. What had she thought then? What had she felt? Was it really part of her own life?

As she always did, for reasons she didn't examine, she drove by the apartment complex where they had lived. It had undergone nearly a dozen renovations; and she wouldn't have recognized it if she hadn't visited three or four times a year, but coming slowly in stages as they had done, each successive façade blended with the past, and Ella was unable to summon a mental image of what it had been when she and Ty lived there.

But she could see their lives during their time here very clearly. She pulled into the parking lot, found a space, drew a deep breath, leaned back in her seat, closed her eyes, and began to live again that long ago life.

It was a new complex then, smelling of new carpet and fresh paint, the latest appliances, a tennis court. It was young, as they were. They lived on the top floor, not minding climbing the stairs because from their kitchen window they could see the Chicago skyline, stately yet pulsing with energy. They shared breakfast every morning looking out toward that near horizon.

Ella fried eggs and bacon, or made biscuits and sausage gravy, or pancakes, or French toast, while Ty talked about his day, his firm, his coworkers and clients. But when she sat down across from him to eat, the conversation turned to things they shared – learning to play tennis, new furniture for the apartment, should they buy a car, did they want a child, would Ella want a teaching job when she finished her doctorate. They kissed, she walked him to the door, they kissed again, and he would leave for his day. Ella knew she would hear every detail about it in the evening. Her day, more mundane, comprised mostly of reading and writing, seemed to yield nothing to talk about.

"I love you, Ella."

"I love you, Ty."

Leaned back, her face in the morning sunlight, Ella relaxed into those long ago moments, and found the shadow of the only passion she'd ever known. Ty was passionate about everything. Ella was passionate only about Ty. The rest – her days of study, casual friends she'd made along the way, her interests and her past – were little more than tiny adornments for a life built around Ty.

How long had it been before it all went away? She could never remember this number, had to calculate it anew every time she thought about it.

She traced back in memory.

They planned to meet at Marshall Fields to choose furniture for their living room, or rather, Ty would watch as Ella chose furniture because she had an unexpected flair for decorating and all things arty. Then they'd have dinner someplace on State Street, someplace they hadn't been before, someplace they'd pick on the spur of the moment.

Ella arrived at the department store about an hour ahead of Ty's expected time so she could browse without commentary. Although she treasured Ty's scattered monologues when they were together, she still did her best thinking in the quiet. Besides, the choosing came first, from some place of intuition and visual imagination inside her, and the rationalization delivered to Ty would be constructed later.

She wandered through their selection, touching fabrics here and there, winding through, around, and back again, eliminating the majority of possibilities almost instantly, allowing her choice to be revealed to her by the number of times she found herself coming back to the same piece. It was cream colored with a high camel back, wooden bun feet, bench seat, no cushions, substantial, simple, timeless, able to accommodate nearly any style or color she might choose to accompany it. She stroked the upholstery, trying to get a sense of whether it would soil easily, whether it would be comfortable to bare skin, not too slick and cold, not too nubbly and abrasive. She sat down on it and scooted her butt to the back, evaluating whether a person could sit comfortably with feet on the floor or feet on a table or feet on the sofa itself. A saleswoman approached her, but Ella shooed her away saying she was waiting for her husband, lying that he would make the decision. She didn't want someone else's patter confusing her thinking, which, as yet was still outside words. Ella resumed her wandering to make sure she hadn't missed anything and began to think about the time.

Ty was late, which wasn't too unusual. Being a junior partner, the structure of his day was very often beyond his control. Ella occupied herself by looking at dishes. Then table linens, bed linens, bath linens. Lamps, statues, bric-a-brac, appliances. Periodically, she would circle back through furniture to see if he was waiting for her and browsing on his own. Cookware, flatware, gadgets, throw pillows, bed pillows, shams, duvets. She was finding it difficult not to worry, her shopping had become little more than pacing around displays that had become obstacles. She knocked a couple things from shelves, replaced them, collected herself, studied a china pattern, returned to her sofa choice.

Standing there, intent and yet unfocussed, she saw Ty's face. Clearly it appeared before her though he was not in the store.

"I love you." And he was gone. There was no more.

Ella screamed and fell back onto the sofa that was to be theirs. Gathering herself, trying not to sob, she ran from the store, hailed a taxi, and made her way home through a blur of panic, traffic, and twilight. She rushed up the stairs to their apartment, unable to catch her breath, or manage a steady gait. Opening the door onto the darkness, she stood for a moment, hoping he was here, knowing he wasn't, knowing he would never be here again.

Finally, collecting herself for the third time that evening, she stumbled out of her shoes, went to her chair at the table by the kitchen window and sat down to wait. All through the night, Josie waited. In the near dawn, before the sky went lavender and pink, when the blackness gave way to sullen then silver gray, the hospital rang for Ella.

194

"Ella? Mrs. Tyson Dillard?"

"Yes."

"I'm sorry to tell you your husband has been involved in an accident."

"Is he…"

"He is here. He is alive. But his injuries are severe. We can send one of our volunteers for you. Would you like us to do that?"

"Yes."

TY'S GHOST

PARKED in the lot where their first and only home had been, for the thousandth time Ella remembered that day, each time remembering it more clearly than the time before. Even though the actual living of it was a blur, the memories were crystalline.

Ty, still and pale, lay with his head bandaged and a single IV drip into his left arm. Ella had expected buzzing, beeping machines, ventilators, monitors, bags of blood for transfusion. She had expected casts, splints, supports, stitches. There was none of that. Other than a single small bandage at the back of his neck and some puffiness in his face, she could see nothing that indicated severe injury. Except for the eerie silence, she might have felt relieved.

Taking his right hand in hers, she sank into the chair beside his bed. It would be fine now. They were together. They would always be together. It would be fine. Sooner or later, maybe after a difficult recovery, maybe after some changes in their plans for the future, maybe after some adjustments, but sooner or later, eventually, they would be fine. They had to be fine.

Nurses came into and out of the room, checking his vital signs, promising Ella a visit from his doctor who would explain everything. Someone told her to eat the tray of food mistakenly sent by the cafeteria for Ty and she supposed she had. She'd used his restroom a time or two. She dozed and she waited.

It was when the doctor flicked on the light that Ella became fully awake. She stood at attention, summoning everything within her to focus. It was useless. She grasped only disjointed words here and there: …hematoma… …massive… …cerebral cortex… …relieved pressure… …damage… …too soon to tell… …physically healthy… …go home and rest…

It took more than weeks or months; it took the passage of years into decades for Ella to grasp completely the doctor's meaning, perhaps because he was uncertain himself of the implications. When Ty regained consciousness, Ella was again sure that everything would be fine. And again when he was able to recognize changes in his environment, when he looked with purpose at someone entering the room, when he could swallow food from a spoon. Ella was sure there would be a time, an eventually, when everything would be fine.

Once the blood bubble had seeped its contents back into his system, all therapies were vigorously undertaken. Ella would visit Ty and hear the staff rejoice: Ty held his own cup and didn't spill his milk today! Ty dressed himself today! Ty walked with a walker today! Ty nodded yes when asked if he wanted a cookie! Ty could point to the correct picture on the board when given its name! He knew "cup", "fork", "window", "bed"…

"Has he spoken?" Ella asked.

"No. But that doesn't mean he never will!"

Ty was dismissed from the hospital to a long term residential care facility, the nicest one Ella could find. And there, physical therapy, occupational therapy, speech therapy continued. There was music and entertainment and activities. The only thing absent was progress.

Time ambled by, a slow, steady, aimless pace. Days were filled with activities much akin to those that occupied preschoolers. Rooms filled with bright colors, soft objects, and the cheery voices of therapists who could celebrate tiny incremental gains, because they had not experienced the massive, all-in-a-moment losses. The "before" that Ella had of Ty was very different from the "before" the staff had of him. It was only to be expected that Ty's "after" would be seen in different lights.

Ella wanted some share in their sense of progress, she wanted to think Ty could come back to her, that he wasn't lost to her forever. She visited Ty every day while she worked on completing her doctorate in philosophy, then twice a week as she developed and taught her courses at the community college. She would go in the early morning, during breakfast, hoping to jar some memory, hoping to start anew over bacon and eggs, hoping for any starting point, no matter how far back, no matter how much might remain to be travelled.

He would smile at her when she sat to join him, patiently allow someone to tie an oversized bib around his neck, eat whatever was fed to him with neither enjoyment nor disdain, and look vacantly about between bites. Ella talked to him about her day, her studies, her work, her new hobbies. Sometimes, for the briefest of moments, his eyes would connect with hers, and she would look for his soul, wondering if it was still inside him, or if it had left in that moment she sat on the sofa in Marshall Fields and saw his face before her. "I love you," she would say. And he would smile.

She couldn't tell if Ty was still in there, if some part of him was sharing space in his skull with the pressurized bubble of blood that had bloomed and receded. What was left of him? Was it that he couldn't hear or that he couldn't respond? Was it that he couldn't recognize her face or didn't remember he had a wife? That was the first pressing question: What was left of Ty? The second question was: Would there ever be more?

The meal complete, the I-love-you spoken, an aide would come and wheel him away to begin his day's activities and Ella would leave to begin hers.

Was it weeks? Months? Years? How many? She couldn't recall. Why was it that one day, not a special day, after one visit, not a special visit, that she asked her question outright? To whom had she directed the question? An aide? A therapist? A doctor? She couldn't recall. The response, however, imprinted itself indelibly.

"Will he ever speak as Ty?"

Clad in hospital attire, a freckled young face, pixie haircut, wide green eyes, the worker, whatever her credentials might have been, looked directly at Ella, stunned speechless. In that moment, Ella knew. She knew she had asked a painfully ludicrous question. It was taboo to ask because the answer was a foregone conclusion that could never be spoken.

Though she spoke it aloud, Ella answered only for herself, "No. He never will."

After that revelation, a deep certainty she had long craved, there were days when Ella almost wished Ty dead, that he had bled out right there on the street, that the ambulance had picked up a dead corpse instead of a living one. At the very least, she wanted it to become clear in everyone's mind that Ty was dead and that the person they ministered to was a ghost.

ELLA LEARNS NEW THINGS

SHE WANTED TO MOVE ON with her life, but she wasn't sure how much life was left to her. Ella desperately missed the passion Ty had brought to her life. Without him, she was unable to sustain it. She wanted to feel love or excitement or hatred or anger. She needed to feel something, but there was nothing. Ty could not be her love and excitement. He had been hit in a crosswalk by an underage driver fleeing the police; and the driver himself was killed when he hit the lamppost a split second later. So there was no one to hate. That left anger as the only available emotion. But no available object was allowed for it.

She didn't know what to do with herself. She couldn't get it sorted out in her own mind. What had she lost? She had Ty, or his shadow or ghost or remnant. Was she or was she not widowed? She had their apartment, her job, sufficient means, and no life, nothing to fill her off-work moments, nothing to care about, no one to go home to, no one to infuse her life with plans and passions and brightness. She had time. Probably years of it.

Never a gifted teacher, Professor Ella Dillard's courses had become lethargic and perfunctory, but, sadly, those are not necessarily negatives in the academic world. She was predictable and steady. She covered all the bases. Students knew what to expect. They left her courses uninspired, but not dissatisfied –

which corresponded exactly with her own feelings about her job. In other words, she was the kind of female faculty member that departments, and especially male colleagues, saw as ideal: she did the job, didn't say much, and was no competition or threat to anyone else's aspirations. For her part, she neither loved nor loathed her job, and never thought in terms of career or vocation. Thoughts of campus, curricula, colleagues, or students rarely crossed her mind after five in the evening. That time had been full of Ty. And now, there was nothing.

But she couldn't just sit. As a child, Ella had wandered the fields and woods of Mac County, gathering poke greens, lambs quarter, wild spinach and leeks in early spring, black berries in July and wild grapes in August. She picked persimmons, dug sassafras roots, and collected hazel nuts, walnuts, and pecans in the late fall. Her father, Monroe, had shown her the gifts nature offered, unaided and unasked, straight from the wild, when she was so young she couldn't remember him doing it. Much later it must have been, Monroe showed her how to ride, entrusting his daughter to an old mare who knew more than Ella did, until Ella had learned enough to teach something to a younger horse. In the outdoors, wildcrafting, horseback riding, and reading were all that she knew to do. Of these, only reading was a reasonable activity to transfer to the middle of Chicago. She needed more. Just to fill the time, she needed more.

Sorting through her mail, a job she performed only monthly, and then for the sole purpose of paying her bills, immediately tossing as junk mail everything that wasn't in an envelope, a small catalog caught her eye when it fell from the overflowing trashcan. It was from her own college and contained descriptions of continuing education courses. When she hadn't been with Ty, the only places Ella had ever felt at home were in the wilderness of Mac County and on college campuses. Mac County didn't seem a viable option, but she was on campus every day. She decided to enroll in something the next day, and she didn't much care what it would be. She didn't even page through the catalog. Indeed, she didn't even retrieve it from the floor.

By the time Ella remembered she wanted to sign up for courses, it was late in the day. She hurried over to the registrar's office and reached the window only to realize that she hadn't selected any courses. Embarrassed, but undeterred, she stepped up and declared that she'd like to sign up for two courses, and she preferred those that had the smallest number of students enrolled. The registrar herself came to the window to help when she recognized Ella as a faculty member. She scrolled through her listing of courses, finally announcing that Beginning Weaving had only ten students signed up so far, and Gun Safety and Beginning Sharp Shooting had only seven each. Ella signed up for all three. The registrar, assuming this was some type of research project, asked if her department should be billed. "No, I'll pay for them," Ella said. And it was done. The evenings became doable. Summer became doable.

It turned out that weaving suited Ella very much. It was solitary, required physical exertion, and offered an artistic outlet she hadn't even realized she needed. By the second week of class, she was ready to venture out on her own. She began scouring Chicago and the surrounding area for floor looms. The hunt itself was pure joy.

As for the shooting, she was a natural.

ELLA COMES HOME

AN ETERNITY OF BLANDNESS dragged by over the next several years, Ella drifting along on a lifeless routine of Ty visits, teaching, weaving, and shooting. Then, unexpectedly, as is the way of irony, it was death that granted her resurrection. Her parents died within two weeks of one another, her father succumbing to old age and her mother succumbing to grief. Old fashioned as they were, having one another to completely fill their worlds, they had been satisfied with the mail correspondence they had with their daughter. They saw their relationship with her as an affectionate and loving relationship, and as all that could reasonably be expected over a distance as great as the one between Chicago and MacDonald County.

As sole heir to their acreage, and they owned nothing more, Josie decided to go home. She had never loved Chicago and she had only tolerated teaching. She didn't want to be Ella anymore. For a young man, Ty had been amply invested and insured. Though certainly not rich, money wasn't a problem. Her needs were simple – and about to get much simpler.

It was a full section of hills, flint rock, and timber that had been her parents' place. There was a beautiful little creek that ran through it which made it home to abundant wildlife. About forty acres or so had been cleared, surrounded by sturdy fence, and sown with fescue. The rest was left untouched. It had a good well and the sturdy log house her father had built. This much she remembered. She felt no need to visit before she moved in.

Ella hired an architect in Chicago to draw up plans for a modest update, and allowed his firm to make arrangements to have the work completed. She received all drawings and photos showing the progression of the work via email and fax, pronounced her satisfaction, and paid for the work, without ever setting foot on the place. She gave detailed instructions to her movers regarding the placement of her looms and furniture, and how the contents of her cabinets should be arranged.

Her plan was to move into her old childhood home and take up her new adult life – erasing the interim by minimizing the transition. At the close of her last day as a professor of philosophy, she intended to go to her car, drive to Mac County, walk into her childhood home, unpack two suitcases, and commence her new life without further ado.

Somewhere between Chicago and Mac County, she decided that she was Monroe and Goldie's daughter come back to them, when really, it was quite the reverse. Monroe and Goldie had come back to their daughter. She had scarcely thought of them in more than a decade. Indeed, she had mourned but little when they passed. They had not been close as Ella defined such things. She was not joined to the beating of their hearts as she had been with Ty's heart. With Ty, she had longed to be a body within a body, a heart within a heart, to become a sweet amalgam of oneness – but their time together had been too short. Their day had been only a morning.

It was driving along I-44, the Saint Louis Arch in view, that she realized her parents had shared with one another exactly the love she had hoped to achieve with Ty, and they had seen it through to its full glory. It came to her that she believed such love with Ty was possible because she had already witnessed its splendor in the old hand hewn log house in Mac County.

For Ella her parents were a comfy chenille robe, worn and dingy – around her, yet apart from her, warming but not intimate, relied upon, yet easy to forget. Of course, they were sufficient to one another. Of course, they needed no other piece to complete the picture of their lives. In this light, it became understandable that her parents had neither the need nor the inclination to dote upon their only child. Care. They cared for her. Love? Perhaps. But if their love for one another was the noon day sun, their love for Ella was the wan daybreak of early spring. Their daughter must take that and build brightness for her own life with her own love.

But it had not worked that way for her. Whatever promise of brightness Ty held was quenched entirely in a pedestrian crosswalk twenty years ago.

Ella cried the rest of the way home. It wasn't grief exactly, not any one thing of remarkable intensity, it was a collage of pastel emotions against a gray of disappointment – a sweet nostalgia for her girlhood and her parents, a soft remembrance of the short space of time with Ty, a hollow sense for her lonely years in Chicago. All these things were lost and gone and only numb confusion filled the void. She had a profound feeling of being lost in the world, as if her own existence had somehow been misplaced.

She hoped there was more to learn, a new noon-day sun, a path back to herself to be found in her childhood home in Mac County. And even if there were not, she had no other ideas about what she might do with the rest of her life.

By the time she reached Joplin, her crying had mostly abated as she had to consider the tangle of old half remembered county highways and dirt roads that would lead her home. Even well south of town, things had not yet begun to look familiar. It had been a very long time.

She had been a different person. In college, with Ty, and in her career in Chicago, she had been Ella. To her parents here in Mac County, she had been Josie.

And she could feel herself becoming Josie again as something inside her, something without words, steered her car into a driveway with an old hand hewn log cabin at the end of it.

Josie was home.

FOLLOWED

CECIL AND SONNY WATCHED from across the street as Josie leaned her seat back and seemed to doze in the parking lot of an aging apartment complex. They had surmised between them that she was here to meet cohorts in crime of some sort, and had been stood up. They found themselves both disappointed and relieved. In the time they'd been waiting and feeding one another's imaginations, they both realized that it was possible they might find themselves in over their heads. They agreed it would be best to simply follow her and not get themselves involved in any of her escapades, no matter what they might be. Given that Josie's reservation was for only a single night's stay, they agreed that it would be safer, and very likely more productive, to follow her today, stay another night, and retrace their steps tomorrow, stopping to ask questions – as any undercover detective would likely do. This change in plans meant only that Cecil would have to call his mother and ask to keep her car another day. Sonny had to answer to no one.

The first thing they had to remember the next morning is that they had not followed Josie Mansell. Instead, according to her hotel registration that Cecil had pilfered several weeks ago, and according to everyone they talked to, here in Chicago they were following Ella Dillard. Information was shockingly easy to obtain from everyone they talked to – mostly because no one knew the slightest reason to hide anything. Surprisingly, Sonny had a gregarious side, an absolutely charming smile – and it didn't hurt that he was very beautiful physically. Cecil found himself in the position of mostly taking notes, and forced himself to view this as the more important aspect of their investigation.

After Ella stopped at the old apartment complex, an interlude her followers were never able to explain, she drove an hour through the middle of Chicago, along a route she managed with notable skill and familiarity, to a rundown care facility. Later, a description of her to the staff, an unprofessional and chatty group, yielded the information that her husband was a longtime resident. From there, Ella drove to a neighborhood post office, and retrieved mail that appeared to be related to financial assets, insurance policies, and professional communications, the first of these undoubtedly related to her husband's current situation. They were evidently routine in nature, as Ella threw them unopened into the back seat of her rental car.

It was mid-afternoon when Ella drove to an art gallery in the Lincoln Park neighborhood. She was greeted with an enthusiastic hug from a woman slightly younger than herself, and escorted inside. After an hour or so, both women returned to Ella's car, opened the trunk and retrieved woven rugs and wall hangings. It was only too late that Cecil and Sonny learned Ella and the woman had exited through a different part of the building. They were gone for several hours. When they returned, Ella got in her car and went back to the hotel.

Their later visit with the woman, who turned out to be the owner of the gallery, provided a treasure trove of information. Ella was her sister-in-law. Tess was every bit as talkative as her brother once was; and Sonny's single casual question regarding one of the wall hangings opened the way for an extended and animated conversation.

"Yes, that is an exceptionally beautiful and innovative weaving! It's all natural hand-dyed wool. Isn't the red exquisite? I don't know anyone who has managed to get such true-to-life colors as Ella has! And her designs are her own. Never two pieces alike, yet every single one is Ella through and through. Have you seen this one over here? As with every artist of merit, it is her emotions that bleed through into her art and give it life, don't you think?"

Sonny expertly feigned interest in the artist, his gift of gab being nearly as great an asset as his good looks. Tess found his accent charming, in spite of the fact that she allowed him scant opportunity to use it.

"Yes, I do know the artist very well! She's my sister-in-law. Well, let's see. What can I tell you about her...? She has a doctorate in philosophy and taught for many years here in Chicago. But that life can become quite tiring and I think Ella yearned for an artistic outlet. You know? Anyway, she moved down south somewhere, Missouri I believe, but it could be Arkansas. I never can remember exactly. Not that it matters. As I understand it she's become quite the farmer!"

Tess giggled and continued.

"I just can't imagine Ella with a horse and sheep and a garden and all that! But she says it sustains her and informs her art – and I guess it does. Just look around you!"

Tess continued her non-stop chatter till Cecil claimed they were late for another appointment and had to leave. Once back in Cecil's mother's car, they realized to their unspoken shame that they had quite forgotten they believed Josie to be a murderess, having been overtaken by plain old nosiness. They each laid the fault to Tess who distracted them with the unexpected unimpeded velocity of her speech. Indeed, they felt a little dizzy.

They thought there would likely be little else of relevant interest for them to discover in Chicago; but they decided to check the last stop Josie made before leaving town the day before. They found they were quite wrong about its importance. Her last stop before leaving Chicago and heading back south proved to be the most damning – at least to Cecil's and Sonny's way of thinking.

Ella had driven to the campus where she'd worked as a faculty member, and entered their athletics building. Finding out what she had done there was surprisingly difficult given how easily they'd acquired access to her affairs everywhere else. But it was well worth their effort and they were rewarded for their diligence.

There were no signs marking the way, no helpful relatives, no information desk. There were hallways and stairways and locked doors, and finally, blessedly, one very bored ancient janitor lackadaisically pushing a dust mop and hoping something would pull him away from the task.

The two approached him and, dropping all pretense of subtlety, doubting it would be necessary in this case, named and described Ella, and asked if he'd ever seen her around. Cecil thought it best that he do the talking here.

"Once in awhile. Why?"

"We're former students." Not an innovative lie, but they didn't need much.

"She uses the firing range."

"The firing range?!"

"I thought you said you were former students."

"Uh…"

"But now that I think of it, most students probably don't even know it's down here. I know a lot of the faculty don't know about it."

"That's right. We didn't know. Our friends didn't know."

"That's 'cause you weren't in ROTC. It was built for the ROTC way, way back. Years ago. I guess most people just forgot it was here."

He leaned in confidentially, "'Spite of what people think, most professors aren't the brightest bulbs in the box – if you know what I mean."

He went on. "But that Doctor Dillard, she's different. She's just like ordinary folks. She's not much of a talker, but she don't put on airs."

"Who runs the firing range?"

"That'd be Steve. He's in charge. Does a lot of shooting himself and one of the few faculty members interested in keeping the range open – so they gave it to him to keep! It's not much trouble these days and I don't think he minds too much. But if you want to see it, you'll have to ask him. He's the only one I know of with keys to it. When he needs it cleaned up, he has to let me in."

"I think we would like to see it. Is Steve around?"

"Last I saw him, he was headed toward his office. It's just around the corner down this hallway here. It's the only office down there."

The two left the janitor to his mopping and his boredom and headed in the direction of Steve. Finding him shuffling through papers on his desk with about as much enthusiasm as the janitor mustered for his mop, they knocked on his door.

"Yep."

"We're former students of Doctor Dillard's and we were looking for her – "

They were cut off. He didn't even look up from his paper scavenger hunt.

"Well, you screwed up your calendar and missed her. She was here early this morning."

"She comes here to shoot?"

"Are you students or biographers?"

"We're just curious. She had a big impact on our lives."

"Really? Well, I guess everyone influences someone. Yes. She comes here to shoot. It's a shooting range. If someone comes here, they come to shoot. That's why it's called a shooting range."

"Is Doctor Dillard...?"

They were cut off again. "If you're asking if she's a good shot, the answer is yes. One of the best I've ever seen. A natural. If you want to know what she shoots, the answer is anything that will fire a load. If you want to know anything else, you're in the wrong office."

They left, knowing they would only be remembered as part of a blur of faces forever associated with interruption and stupidity. And they didn't care. They had finally discovered something interesting! They had been real detectives!

It was a quiet drive home. They didn't know what to make of it. They had learned so much about Josie; and yet they had learned nothing at all about whether, why, or how she killed her neighbors. This problem hadn't occurred to them till the moment it arose: What does a person do with information once they've got it? By the time Cecil dropped Sonny off and drove home, both young men had made their decisions – and they were very different from one another.

Cecil analyzed his notes and decided that he needed much more to convince CB that he had anything at all. More importantly, he allowed himself to acknowledge that if what he'd been doing came to light, CB would likely be very displeased. He might even get fired over it. Some tiny voice of wisdom inside him said it was better to be permitted to play the part of law enforcement officer, than to be fired for actually trying to be one.

Sonny, on the other hand, had nothing to win or lose. He knew murder wasn't a rarity, especially in Mac County. What if Tiger or Huck, or even Jay, had been shot first? What if Duke and Newt had been shot first? Wouldn't the condition of the corpses hide the gunshot? What if someone knew enough about herbs to poison pot? What if Cecil was onto something? As they say in the country: even a blind squirrel finds a nut every now and then. So, the very next morning, Sonny took all his "knowns" and "what-if's" and went to the best and wisest man he knew. He took them to Jack.

TWILIGHT

THE EVENING AFTER she returned from Chicago, at
the very moment of twilight, when the mournful call
of doves had gone silent, and the sweet hopeful cries
of whippoorwill found their spaces in the silence,
before the cries of owls, crickets, and cicadas had
begun, Josie whistled for Selah. It was unnecessary and
they both knew it. He had been waiting for some time
now, head over the fence, eyes and ears alert, waiting
for her and their evening ride. She could not help but
see, as she did every day, that her gelding was still
beautiful, despite his advancing age. At sixteen years,
he was still sound, strong and straight of leg and back;
but how many years did he have left? Black as a colt,
fading over time to blue roan, and now to a fine dapple
gray, still very dark in his mane and tail, to Josie's eye
he had become stately and dignified in appearance,
matured and elegant. He still moved well, though
perhaps not as quickly. Her father would have said that
he was too big to be a woman's horse, but Josie loved
his power and his size, his eminence.

She opened the gate, greeted him with a pat on
the cheek, and put on his bridle. But instead of leading
him through the gate to the other side of the fence for
their usual ride, she leaned back against the nearest
fence post, unable to decide what to do next. A feeling
of impending change washed over her, as if to warn her
that this moment in time was only a moment, that it

was singular, that there may not be many more, or perhaps any more, like it, that life was moving forward, and that eventually it would do so without her, that she and Selah would be gone and that only doves, whippoorwills, frogs and the bugs would be left behind.

Selah had not grown gray alone. Josie took her single braid, brought it around her neck, and stared at it. Finding it mostly gray, she turned her hand palm side down and looked at the skin on the back, the skin of an old woman – thin, spotted, speckled, wrinkled. She dropped the braid. Touching her face now, she ran her fingers lightly over the web of creases around her eyes, nose, and mouth. None of this was surprising to Josie. It was more clinical assessment than emotional catharsis, more akin to checking the weather forecast than fearing a funeral. It was a moment of cool acknowledgment – both Selah and Josie had become "long in the tooth".

She shrugged it off.

It had been an oppressively hot day, even for the Ozarks in August. She didn't know what the temperature had been, though she was certain it had hit triple digits. Maybe it was too hot for a ride? Maybe she and Selah should take a day off? And do what? What else was there to do? They had grown dependent upon their routine to anchor their days, to take note of the seasons, to be one with each other in the out of doors.

Selah had become impatient, waiting there, whipping his tail, bobbing his head, stomping his feet against the horse flies that had found him standing in one place too long. Josie strapped a horse blanket to his back instead of getting a saddle, climbed the board fence, and mounted from there, no longer agile or strong enough to mount from the ground. Solomon, Josie's very best friend and guardian, roused himself from the cool dirt beside the barn, shook the powdered red clay dust from his coat, wagged his tail a couple times, and joined them as they headed up the driveway to the road.

When the first houses were built along it, and it was not much more than a wide trail, it was named Thrifty Acres Road. Josie thought it was a tacky name and was glad no one remembered it anymore. After a few more houses were built, it was given a number – rural route five – and that is how Josie thought of it. Later, it became Dutch Elm Drive, the post office evidently drawing names out of a hat, because there wasn't an elm tree within a dozen miles. It should have been Red Oak Drive, or Hickory Drive, or Walnut, or Pecan, or Red Cedar Drive. Dutch Elm Drive was just stupid. But it seemed to Josie, now, after all she'd done, now, that her vision seemed to be clearing, now, that feelings were beginning to come back to inform her thinking, that there was no more or less stupidity here, no more or less meanness here, than in other parts of the world, and that those numbers, that average ratio of good, bad, and indifferent, were never likely to change.

But this was home; and home is the place where the meanness, the badness, the pain is more acutely felt because it is more intimately known.

It wasn't always like this. It was as if she had lived never seeing her own reflection, her interactions with the world having been so slight. In this way, Mac County and Chicago had been exactly the same for Josie. She occupied her days differently in each place, saw different people in each place, but she was never a real person either place. Except for when she was with Ty, the before-the-accident Ty, she was not a visible person, even in her own dreams. She was a fallen leaf, a snowflake, a blade of grass, an entity entirely ordinary in every way.

When was it that weaving and listening turned into caring and doing? What was it, exactly, that she had cared about? What had she done?! How could it be that a philosophical puzzle, a moral inquiry, became something else? She believed herself still to be invisible, but she had become aware that she was no longer ordinary. Still, perhaps the biggest change for Josie was that she allowed such thoughts to linger in her mind a little longer. She allowed herself to look at them, and to ponder them as more than hypotheticals. After several decades of life, she was becoming a person in her own right – and she wasn't sure she liked it.

When she left her driveway on Selah, she headed east, away from the downing sun, toward the full and rising moon, into the twilight.

Selah was restless and Josie allowed him a gentle gallop to settle his nerves. Trots were too hard on their old bones for either of them to enjoy it and runs were just exhausting. They walked or cantered these days. Truth to tell, mostly they walked, a gait Selah assumed on his own in less than a quarter mile, and Josie allowed this, too. In her younger days, she imposed her own will in all instances, but saw little need for that anymore. They settled into a cool peaceful amble, sweat evaporating from both of them, and a routine calmness wrapped itself around them. They had done this thousands of times, in all kinds of weather, in every season, evening after evening blending into a timeless whole.

But there had been a handful of special full moon night times. This was going to be one of those night times. Josie had decided what to do and she was going to do it tonight.

For the first time in her life, Josie made a life and death decision that she could explain. At least to herself.

JOSIE BIDS TY FAREWELL

AFTER SHE FINISHED HER RIDE, Josie started her pickup, and left her hand hewn log cabin behind her. She hadn't even bothered to change clothes. Josie drove slowly, cars passing her by unnoticed. By the time she was deep into Chicago's maze of entrance and exit ramps, merge lanes, and traffic cone barricaded construction projects, she would have been a real hazard if had not been the middle of the night and had she not known the route by heart.

She brought nor wore a pencil skirt, silk blouse, stylish heels. Her hair was not upswept into a coil. This time, she came not as Ella, but as Josie – clothed in her usual overalls, her hair in its usual braid.

She did not stop to revisit the apartment complex where she and Ty had loved – where they had lived truly and fully within each other's worlds. That time and place had gone. Neighborhoods had shifted. Over the years, what had once been clean and new with promise, was now covered with untended vines, overgrown hedge, volunteer sprouts of what would never be trees – all these hiding the graffiti predicting what would ultimately obscure it. No one lived there anymore and the day it would be bulldozed to rid the neighborhood of this living death was already marked on the city calendar.

In the morning, she would not be visiting the gallery that sold her rugs. In the afternoon, she would not visit her old campus for a session of target shooting. She had brought neither rugs nor firearms with her.

She came for the same reason she always came to Chicago – to see Ty.

It was as if she saw, for the first time in many years, the assisted living center she had been visiting for decades. Like the apartment complex, it had deteriorated, passing from one owner to the next, each trying to wring more profit from its inhabitants and their families, putting less money into maintenance and care, knowing most families had given up on their loved ones long ago. It might be argued that the inhabitants themselves were little affected by the changes. They lacked the capacity to notice shabbier grounds, less nutritious food, dirtier rooms, irregularly rotated bed linens, discontinued therapies, untrained and smaller staffing, more liberal disbursement of chemical restraints. Despite her many visits, Josie herself had failed to notice these things.

Oblivious for so many years, Josie now took note that she was able to enter through a side door, not only without being questioned, but without being seen. She made her way to his room without encountering a single soul.

When she visited in the past, she had eyes only for Ty. Even then, in her desperate search for what was no longer there, she had become blind to what was. It was impossible for her to understand. She was unable to form a link in her mind between the man she loved – animated, passionate, profoundly alive – with what she saw before her.

In truth, he was a paradox. He had the abilities of a three year old, but lacked the liveliness. He could feed, dress, and toilet himself – so he was no trouble to the staff. But he had no curiosities, no interests, no affections, no desires other than to have his daily routine unperturbed. He neither remembered nor recognized faces, and though he tolerated being touched by others, as his physical care often demanded, he had no reaction to it, neither seeking nor avoiding human interaction of any kind.

He had persisted through bouts of flu and constipation, various skin ailments, and most recently, poorly attended pressure sores, until, as Josie noted with a slight smile, he had grown old, as she had, sharing one last superficial feature – they had both grown gray. She looked more closely now. His hair was much like the rest of him – all thin and gray and brittle. Except for his hair, he had no commonalities with Josie. Through the hard work of weaving and gardening, the recreations of riding and walking, Josie's muscles retained a wiry strength. She was supple and moved with ease and vigor. Her days in the sunshine, her joys and anger, had bestowed upon her face a texture of well-worn leather – lightly tanned, slightly thin, amply wrinkled. In short, she carried upon her body all the signs of a person who had lived. Ty did not. His skin was smooth, sallow; muscles atrophied, joints stiff.

She took his soft hands in her calloused ones, stroked them, hoping against last hope that she would rouse Ty as Ty. She did not. Still holding his hands in one of hers, she took the other and laid it upon his neck just below his jawbone. He was so thin. It was easy to feel the pulsing of his carotid artery, slow and regular. She closed her eyes, seeking some sign of uncertainty within herself. Finding none, she allowed his hands to slip gently from hers back onto the mattress. Still with one hand on his neck, she slipped the other into an overall pocket so deep she almost had to bend to retrieve the knife from its bottom. She grasped it, flipped it open, took a long breath, and slid it across Ty's neck between her hand and his jawbone.

Blood pulsed forth upon his pillow. His heart had not the strength to send shoots into the air. Instead, an ebb and flow of red spent itself onto the bed. Josie waited, still and silent, for it to stop. When it had, she bent over his face and kissed his forehead. His eyes opened for a moment, as if he knew her, as if he thanked her, as if he loved her. He blinked once and when his eyes reopened, it was with the blank stare she had borne so long. Yet there was peace now. Blood had made the peace. Blood. Blood had made the dying – the dying that had been paused and perpetuated for all these years gone. Josie laid her hand upon the blood that covered his neck and then laid it upon her heart. Three times she did this. A ritual of goodbye, of love, of peace. Then, slowly, with a sense of calm and contemplation, she turned, walked the hallway to the side door, and left just in time to greet the dawn of a new day.

She drove back through Chicago and all the way home, breathing deeply, freely, thinking about nothing at all.

JACK TELLS JOSIE A STORY

WHEN JOSIE PULLED INTO HER OWN DRIVEWAY just at dusk, she was surprised to see Jack's pickup there. It was only then she realized that she lived in a world where her actions might not be understood. It was only then she realized that something might come after Ty's death. And that it might not be good. And, worst of all, she cared whether it was good, ached for it to be good.

It was as if she had been shaken from a daze. She saw that her own life had been paused in much the same way Ty's had been. If he had been a compliant three-year-old, she had been not much more than an enraged two-year-old – appearances on both counts notwithstanding.

Neither of them had had life, seeing all of it, feeling all of it, embracing all of it – he, because he could not; she, because she would not.

Now that blood had anointed and confirmed Ty's death, they were both released from limbo, and Josie wanted to live. Whatever time she had left, she really wanted to live it. She wanted to be Josie – fully alive.

Josie didn't know what to do. She had been gone less than twenty-four hours. It had never occurred to her that she might be missed. She allowed her pickup to roll down the drive and coast to a stop next to Jack's. She sat there at the wheel, frantically trying to think what to do. Jack came up to the window which she reluctantly rolled down, still looking straight ahead of her. Placing both forearms on the door, relaxed, normal, as if this were an ordinary chat with a neighbor who'd pulled over on the dirt road for a visit, Jack considered Josie, moving only his eyes, he took in the blood, the tiredness, the probabilities.

After Sonny had shared all his "what-if's" with Jack, Jack determined that he would see if he could get them answered and that there was only one way to do that: directly ask the person most likely to know the answer. He figured that even if the lips lied, the eyes usually didn't, especially when taken by surprise. It didn't take much movement and it took even less time to reveal an entire truth – a single flicker, a tiny momentary narrowing could tell the tale. If there was a serial murderer on the road, Jack had to know. Somehow he felt himself to be a keeper of some kind of order or morality here. It was a job that Jewel had conferred upon him somehow. She loved and cared for so many – and this obliged him to do likewise.

It was late morning by the time Sonny left Jack's place, and it was around noon when Jack pulled into Josie's driveway. He had not expected to have to wait. Gabe had stopped by and left, assuring Jack that Josie had gone to Chicago and that once in a while she'd stay for a couple days. Jack made up his mind to wait till she returned, no matter how long it took. He felt the truth might come easier if Josie was caught unawares and exhausted.

Just as Selah and Soloman were getting restless waiting for their evening ride, once more at the very moment of twilight, Josie's pickup headed into her own driveway.

"Well," he said, quiet calm matter-of-factness saturating his voice, "Looks like ya've had yersef quite an evenin'."

Josie's head dropped to her steering wheel.

"Why'n't cha git yersef outta that pickup, an' we'll figger out whut oughtta come next."

Jack opened the door. Josie turned and slid from the seat. Her knees buckled when her feet hit the dust. Jack caught her under the armpits, set her upright and steered her toward her backdoor. Just inside, he let her drop into the nearest rocker. Final traces of a setting sun bathed the room in subdued and peaceful reds. She closed her eyes and cried, cried like she'd never cried before, great waves of longing and love, regret, grief and relief rolling through her whole body, quietly at first, then rising to peaks, no longer weeping but sobbing, screaming, heaving, finally receding to rocking, humming, and rivulets of tears, until no more movement, sound, or teardrops were possible, a lifetime of these having been spent. She didn't know how much time had passed.

When she caught her breath, she opened her eyes to rediscover Jack, relaxed, rocking back and forth in the chair next to her, looking straight ahead. She was so far beyond exhaustion that she felt nothing but numbness – no surprise, no fear, nothing.

"Tha' was quite a spell. Ya think yer over it?"

"Yes."

"Wanna tell me 'bout it?"

"No."

"Le' me put it 'nother way. It shore as hell look ta me like yer gonna need some hep. An' it don' look ta me like ya gotta lot a places ta git it. Now. I ain't sayin' ah'll hep ya. An', ah ain't sayin' ah won't. All ah'm sayin' is ah'm prob'ly the bes' chance ya got. Start talkin'."

Josie didn't know where to begin and she told Jack so.

"Le' me begin fer ya then. Ya was raised up right here. Ya used ta live in Chicago – where ya went by the name Ella Dillard. Ya use' ta be a college perfesser. Ya have a husban' in a nut house in Chicago. Fer some goddamn reason er other ya started killin' folks here when ya moved back."

Jack knew that, even now, the accusation of killing people in the neighborhood was mostly conjecture. At this point, there wasn't one shred of real evidence that she had had anything to do with anybody's death. Other than the fact that she was secretly a marksman, there wasn't much even to make a person suspicious. In his own mind Jack had to concede that being a marksman and being a murderer are very different things. Owning adjoining land was more trivial yet. Still, Gabe had had some kind of gut feeling for quite a while; and Sonny asked some pretty reasonable questions just yesterday. Most importantly, here she sat before him – an emotional wreck covered in blood that wasn't her own.

Jack waited for Josie's reaction to what he'd put forward as fact. Nothing. He couldn't see anything in her face or movements. She was completely still, staring straight ahead. Jack tried again.

"Not ta say ah'm faultin' yer choices fer makin' dead folks, but ah got frien's – an' ah got ways – an' ya ain't got the secrets from me that ya got from mos' other folks aroun' here."

Jack knew it was mostly bluff, but he didn't have a lot more than that to work with.

"Ah gotta tell ya though, even ole Gabe's got his suspicions these days. Yer turn."

Josie's reaction, without thinking or examination, was to take Jack at his word. She was too tired to think it through. He knew. She didn't know how and it didn't occur to her ask. It had never been in Josie to ask questions. But if Jack knew about Chicago, if Jack knew about Ty, he must certainly know about the rest. She could hardly breathe. It was a puzzle. She herself still wasn't sure how all the pieces fit together. But she had to say something.

Josie didn't look at him. Jack thought she seemed to be talking to herself – as indeed she was.

"I loved him because he was so alive, because he was so different from the quiet ways of my folks, because once he saw me, once he really saw me, I was really here, really in the world myself. With him. I was because he was."

Jack waited, not at all sure what Josie was talking about, knowing that whatever sign he might give wouldn't be observed, and that if it was, she'd likely go back into herself. It was slow going.

"He was walking to meet me. He was hit in a crosswalk by a kid driver. He should have died. The kid did."

Josie paused, her mind grappling with what she was only now catching sight of. She was assembling a puzzle, a map, a meaning, finding her way through her own self, testing it for truth.

"But there wasn't any blood… I never could understand that… He should have bled to death…"

Another long pause. Jack waited, giving no clue as to what might be in his own mind.

"But the blood was all locked in his head… And it killed him… But it wouldn't let him die…"

She seemed to be gaining a clearer view.

"I guess that's how I understand it now. He needed help. He needed help to go ahead and die."

Jack realized that Josie wasn't even talking about anyone in the neighborhood. She was talking about this evening. Looking at Josie, still covered in blood, Jack made a logical guess sound like a known fact.

"So. Ya kilt 'im."

After thinking a moment, Josie corrected Jack, looking at him for the first time:

"No. I let him die."

"Yer purty fuckin' bloody fer someone who's jes lettin' sum-thin' happen. Ya got 'nuf blood on ya that it looks like ya kinda hepped things along."

Josie glared at Jack, and for the first time, became emphatic.

"I helped him because he wasn't there anymore! He was dead years ago but his body didn't know! I let his body know!"

"Ah see…"

They both sat for a moment wandering in their own thoughts.

Jack's thoughts tended toward the more practical. He could turn her in at any time. Or not. He needed to maintain his own choices. He didn't have much respect for the law and for the most part he was never clear on what good prison was supposed to accomplish. He didn't think he could leave a killer loose in the neighborhood. But even now, it wasn't at all certain, no matter what she'd done in Chicago, that she was a murderer in Mac County.

"Why doncha git yersef cleaned up? Go take a shower. Pitch yer clothes, underwear, shoes an' all, out inta the hall. Clean up the shower and the bathroom floor with bleach. Shower again. Clean the shower and bathroom with clean water – no bleach – twice. Put on a clean set of clothes an' throw out another clean set of clothes ta me. Ah'll deal with yer pickup and yer clothes."

It sounded like help. Enough of it sounded sensible for her to assume that all of it was. Being so far from able to think for herself, she did as she was told. Jack had the reputation as help in the neighborhood. So Jack was helping her now, right?

Jack took his time. He wasn't the kind to panic. As soon as he had her bloodied clothes and shoes, Jack threw them in the front of her pickup. He took chainsaw gas from the back of his pickup, poured it on the seats and floorboards of Josie's truck, and set it all on fire. He hung the clean set of clothes from a nearby tree limb so they'd smell of fire. He went to the back of her house, got her hose, turned on the faucet, and returned to the pickup. After the cab of the pickup had mostly burned itself out, he squirted the hose toward the body and bed and around the perimeter of the truck.

When Josie appeared, he told her her story.

"Here's whut happ'n'd. We was sittin' outside smokin' an' ya flipped a butt inta yer pickup on accident – 'er at leas' ya guess tha's whut musta happ'n'd. All ya know fer sure's the damn thing caught fire an' by the time we got the hose goin' the whole insides was burnt up. Them there hangin' on the limb was the clothes ya's wearin' when it happ'n'd. Go put 'em in a basket er whutever ya do with yer dirty stuff."

Josie stood, taking it in, seeing it as the possible defense it was intended to be. How did Jack know what to do?!

"Now! Goddamn it! Do it now!"

She ran to put her stinking smoky clothes in the hamper and ran back. When she returned, Jack finished her story for her, hoping she'd understand.

"Now. Here ya are. Ain't it nice ta be all cleaned up after tryin' to save yer pickup…? Ain't it sad 'bout that ole pickup…? Ain't we both sad that smokin' made us so slow and addle headed…? Ain't we glad it ain't nuthin' more…? Ain't it jes the way fer things ta happen when a couple neighbors spend the night listnin' to bullfrogs and whippoorwills an' watchin' the moon come up an' shootin' the breeze…? Ain't it jes the way…"

Jack waited to see if Josie fully understood his offer and its implications.

"Right…?"

Josie nodded.

"Now ah'm goin' home an' yer gonna go 'bout yer normal bizness. Yer gonna ride er weave er sew er do whutever the hell ya us'ally do. Sooner er later, they's gonna wanna have a chat with ya. Sooner er later, they's gonna come. Yer job is ta be pulite an' hepful an' ermember yer story whut ah jes give ya. Ya ken be sad er not sad when they tell ya he's dead. Under the circumstances, it don' much matter. Either way's believ'ble. Yer job is ta be shocked when they tell ya he's murdered. Don' overdo it. 'Roun' here, folks think murder's more common in Chicago than in Mac County an' is on'y ta be expected. Don' overdo it. Don' tell 'em no more'n whut ah give ya. If they ask more, jes say ya don' know er ya can't think. Don' matter whut they think. On'y matters what they can prove. An' I don' 'spect they's gonna work too hard on it."

Josie nodded.

"Ah'll be back later so's we ken talk 'bout those otha poor bastards ya kilt."

Josie nodded again – providing Jack with more information than he'd been able to obtain all day.

And with that, Jack got in his truck and he left.

THE LAW

THE NEXT DAY, Josie busied herself at her loom by drifting into a mindless lazy tabby weave, a piece good for nothing but to wipe mud off boots at the back door, her thoughts drifting, too, like smoke curling around all the pieces of her life, rendering them visible only through a haze, yet visible to Josie for the first time in her life. The ringing phone on her kitchen counter brought her back to the day, startling her again into thinking how her actions would be perceived by others. She panicked, not knowing whether to answer or not, but decided that she must – sooner or later, she must.

"Hello?"

"Mrs. Dillard?"

"Yes."

"I'm Detective Foley with the Chicago Police Department."

"Yes."

"I'm sorry, but we have bad news about your husband."

The seemingly inevitable pause after such statements ensued. Josie said nothing. Finally, the voice in Chicago resumed.

"Mr. Dillard passed away in the middle of the night."

Josie was lost to a similar conversation two lifetimes away.

"Mrs. Dillard?"

"Yes."

"Um... ...The circumstances of Mr. Dillard's death were unusual..."

"Yes."

"Mrs. Dillard, do you have anyone there with you at the moment?"

Josie felt hypnotized into a similar phone call years ago. She barely heard the questions, coming in and out of the conversation. She tried to focus.

"No. I'm alone."

"Are you okay?"

"Yes."

"Mrs. Dillard, I'm very sorry to tell you that Mr. Dillard was murdered."

Josie's voice was barely audible on the recording being made by the detective. She spoke softly, slowly, as if to herself.

"No. No, he wasn't murdered. He was killed years ago. He was killed in a crosswalk. The young man who killed him died, too."

"Mrs. Dillard, I'm afraid you don't understand. Mr. Dillard was murdered last night in his bed."

"No. No, he wasn't."

"Mrs. Dillard, do you have any other relatives?"

"No."

"Did Mr. Dillard have any other relatives?"

"He has a sister."

"We've already found her. She says there's no one else. Is that correct?"

"Yes."

"Did Mr. Dillard have any enemies?"

"Of course not. Ty has been dead for years."

Embarrassed, perplexed, and exasperated, Detective Foley, had one more question.

"When was the last time you were in Chicago, Mrs. Dillard?"

"I don't do well with dates. Ask Tess. I sold her my weavings."

"My condolences, Mrs. Dillard."

"Thank you."

"Either I, or one of my colleagues, might want to visit with you in person a little later."

"That would be fine."

And the conversation was concluded. Josie stood for a moment after replacing the phone in the cradle, then slowly walked to her loom, sat down, and resumed weaving, once more lost in puzzle pieces and smoke.

JACK COMES BACK

JACK WAITED TILL TWILIGHT, a time when Josie generally had fewer visitors, and knocked on her back door. Josie yelled at him to come in, not because she knew who he was, but because she acknowledged long ago that a screen door would never be any protection against anyone anyway, and she'd be as well off to begin with a welcome.

"Whyn'cha git down here away from that contraption so's we ken have a better talk."

She knew the topic was sufficiently important to warrant her entire attention, so she complied – wishing she had given it more thought, that the smoke hadn't been so thick, that the pieces had been fitted together.

Josie made herself a cup of coffee, Jack packed a bowl, and they both sat down.

"Well…?"

Josie said nothing. Jack thought it might be better to be more direct.

"Dead folks, Josie. Yer gonna tell me 'bout dead folks an' how they come ta be that a'way."

Still nothing.

"Le's start with Reba an' Leroy."

"Well," Josie drew a deep breath, thinking back, trying to make sense of it, wanting to understand, "I think it was a problem about blood. I didn't know it then."

Jack wondered what in the hell this woman was talking about, but thought it best to let her talk now that she'd finally started. He was glad they were rocking side by side, not seeing one another's faces. It appeared she needed that visual space of privacy and he could no longer be sure what his own facial expressions might reveal.

"I thought I was doing good. There was so much killing and dying here and most of the time it seemed like it was the wrong people. I don't know when I started to think that."

He hated it, but Jack knew there had been times when his own thinking ran along those lines. He began to fear that this conversation might raise more questions than it answered.

"There was so much blood when Tiger died. And even more blood when Huck died."

It was impossible for Jack to feel sure whether Josie knew about the blood in the same way all the neighbors did or whether she was the one responsible for drawing it.

"But I thought the world was better, that Mac County was better, once they died."

Jack surprised himself by saying, "So did I."

Josie didn't notice.

"I didn't want Clarice hurt anymore."

Jack wasn't positive, but he knew the doings in the neighborhood, and he was reasonably certain he knew what kind of hurt Josie meant. He thought of Alice as his daughter and he loved her with a passion. He knew what he would do to protect her. He knew what he had done.

"I tried to make it better, to make it good for Clarice. I didn't think I needed blood. I didn't want to think about blood anymore. I didn't want to think about Ty anymore."

Again, Jack was unable to follow the train of Josie's thinking, even in the long pause that followed. Josie took a deep shuddering breath.

"But I almost killed her! I could have killed Clarice! Blood would have been a better marker. You can tell who's died by the blood."

Jack had to know. With the way that Josie wandered, he might not get this close again. He had to ask. If it wasn't Josie, he would have to find who did it.

"Josie, didja kill Reba with bad weed er not?!"

Josie was startled. She knew she had been slow, but she thought she was being as plain to Jack as she was becoming to herself. Josie and Jack looked directly at one another. Josie told him what she believed he already knew.

"Yes."

Jack pushed forward.

"Where'd ya git the weed?"

"With Tess. In Chicago. About a year ago. I smoke some. Not very often. But I like to have it around so I can."

"Do ya know whut was in it?"

"Hemlock."

"An' ya put it there ya-sef?"

Josie frowned, not understanding why Jack was asking for answers she thought he already knew, and for details she thought were trivial.

"Yes!"

"An' ya shot Tiger and Huck afore they's pulled to pieces – so's they'd be pulled to pieces."

"Yes."

Jack sat for a few minutes longer, stood, stretched, sighed, and left.

Detective Foley never gave Josie another thought except to conclude she was so crazy she wasn't worth their trouble to investigate – and, in any case, that was likely her only guilt.

Always Twilight

JOSIE NEVER GAVE ANOTHER THOUGHT to Detective Foley either.

To all outward appearances, her life was the same as it had always been. She wove and she listened. She tended to her herb gardens and her vegetables. She kept her livestock and herself fed. She rode Selah and hugged Solomon.

Jewel kept Jack busy tending to animals, kids, and old people she dragged home. He continued to make his willow furniture as a visible source of honest income in order to cover the illegal income that enabled Jewel's generosity.

And a year or more passed just so.

He thought about it from time to time, but it was easy to push it away, and in truth, he was mostly called away by the tasks at hand. It was Gabe that brought things front and center again. He had come to Jack's to trade tractor work for meat, an exchange Jack was always happy to make.

"Jack, do ya 'mind way back when ah to'd ya 'bout Josie, an' ah wuz a-worryin' 'bout all 'em dead folks in the neighborhood?"

Jack nodded, but didn't look up from his beer.

"Well. Lookin' like ya was right. Ain't been no dead folks in quite a spell now. No dead folks, no bad dead folks er good dead folks. Ah reckon them wuz jes pecul-yer coincidences back then after all."

Gabe appeared glad to have this off his chest, as if confessing to a false betrayal of a friend.

But Jack simply couldn't rid himself of a nagging hum in the back of his head. If Gabe was this relieved to be confessing to thinking murder, maybe confessing to the real thing would be even better.

Jack decided to pay Josie a visit.

Again, he chose an evening when Josie's visitors had all gone home. It's as if twilight is the honest time of day, a time when subdued colors coalesce to form sharp silhouettes, a time when dark truths are revealed, and then abide till they are softened by moonlight. He found her outside leaning against her board fence, talking to her horse and stroking her dog, surrounded by a rural quiet floating upon the sounds of bullfrogs, whippoorwills, and night bugs. She must have heard him, because she turned to see who was coming at this hour. She smiled, and to Jack, it seemed sweet somehow.

"Josie, we gotta talk."

"Okay."

"Josie, 'bout them killins... ...er dyins ...er them there bleedin's out..."

"Yes."

"Whut was them about?"

Josie sighed, peace and resignation washing over her. She had lived a very good year, really lived it. An ordinary peaceful kind of living, accompanied by an extraordinary awareness that she, Josie, was living these things. It was more than she expected. For most of her life, it was more than she knew to expect. Let come what may – she had lived this past year – and how long was not important. There is a lifetime in a moment if the moment is truly lived. She had lived a lifetime of passion with Ty, and a lifetime of peace since he died.

"I already told you I killed Reba. And I'm responsible for Leroy."

She sighed again and went on.

"I killed Tiger and I killed Huck."

She paused and took a breath.

"And I helped Ty's body know it was dead."

Josie seemed unmoved by her confession, as if there were no difference between the silence and the telling. Jack looked at her from a turmoil inside himself so powerful he seemed to be in pain. He pronounced two names.

"Duke. An' Newt."

"I didn't have anything to do with those."

"Ah did."

"You did what?" Josie was bewildered.

"Ah'm the one whut kilt 'em."

Josie looked away from Jack, back again into her pastures and the moonlight.

"Ain't cha gonna ask why?"

"Not unless you want me to."

"Cuz they wuz a plague on the world. 'Cuz a whut was dun ta little girls like Alice. An' cuz a whut was dun with ma mama's stuff. An' cuz a the hurt of a lot a other folks, too."

"I understand, Jack."

Jack wanted her to look at him, to see her face, to look in her eyes, to read her judgment.

"Whut we dun. Ah don' know 'bout it. Ah'm afeer'd these days, that whut ah use'ta think wuz good, might a'been as bad as whut ah wuz tryin' ta kill. It's been on ma min'. Ah'm thinkin' ah don' even know whut's good an' whut's bad no more."

Jack had confided in Josie more than he ever had with any living person, even his wife, and he felt vulnerable and small. He felt a profound need for help, the kind of help that only someone who had murdered might be able to offer.

"Ah'm askin' whut cha think."

Josie searched for words, words to voice her own newly found understandings. She paused so long Jack almost gave up.

"Jack, I don't know anything about good or bad or right or wrong. And I'm just now beginning to figure out death. And life. I don't have any answers for either one of us. I'm sorry."

Seeing Jack's distress, she tried again.

"Jack, I don't think either one of us made the world a better place. But, for whatever it's worth, I don't think we made it a worse one either."

And that was the peace they had to settle for. Along with night sounds at twilight and the soft sweet smell of persimmon groves, and all suchlike consolations afforded to the truly living.

THE END

About the Author:

The author lives as a semi-hermit on a small farm in the middle of a big woods on the precise edge of nowhere.

She loves sheep and all things fiber. She loves rosemary and all things herbal. She loves the sound of wolves, chickadees, and the wind in the pines.

She loathes bill collectors and all things financial. She loathes mirrors and all things superficial. She loathes mosquitos, gnats, and tech support.

She's mostly neutral about everything else.